SHATTERED

The Lifestyle Trilogy

An erotic novel by

R M Conté

TotalRecall Publications, Inc.
1103 Middlecreek
Friendswood, Texas 77546
281-992-3131   281-482-5390 Fax
www.totalrecallpress.com

ISBN: 978-1-59095-495-9
UPC: 6-43977-44955-9

Printed in the United States of America with simultaneous printing in Australia, Canada, and United Kingdom.

FIRST EDITION
1   2   3   4   5   6   7   8   9   10

Edited by: Sigrid Macdonald
Cover Photo by Kari Hilton Photography
This is a work of fiction. The characters, names, events, views, and subject matter of this book are either the author's imagination or are used fictitiously. Any similarity or resemblance to any real people, real situations or actual events is purely coincidental and not intended to portray any person, place, or event in a false, disparaging or negative light.

Dedicated to those who understand that entertainment comes in many forms.

-R

Dedicated to my mother, whose strength and courage through unspeakable suffering is an inspiration to all blessed enough to know her.

-M

Acknowledgment

Once again, a team rallied 'round to help us bring this book, and the trilogy, to completion. We must thank Kari Hilton Photography, model Kelly Bisceglia, and makeup artist Andrea Gelman. Their proficiency brought our cover to life. Thanks to Frank and Steve for their financial advice and Jillian for her artistic ability. Again, we thank Sigrid, our editor; TotalRecall Press; our publisher; John, who wears many hats for us; and all the readers who continue to support The Lifestyle Trilogy. Lastly, thank you Tim for spending an afternoon on my patio, providing libations and sharing with me your golf expertise. Stay tuned to see what we write next – we're not done yet!

The Book

Beth is newlywed and ready to begin the rest of her life. Her hasty marriage to Don, a wealthy businessman, both shocks and worries Beth's friends with good reason.

Selling her home in Ohio and preparing to move her children to a mansion on Biscayne Bay with Don, turns her world upside down. Following several poor decisions, she is forced to head to the Big Apple to begin a new job. Her many friends, some with good intentions while others negatively influencing her, stimulate Beth's love of swinging. They encouraging her to often visit an exclusive night club catering to all, including celebrities, who need their fantasies and fetishes fulfilled.

Follow Beth's journey from "I do" down a slippery slope of drugs, kink, promiscuity, and the ultimate betrayal.

Can Beth survive the ramifications of The Lifestyle she has chosen?

Chapter 1

Beth felt her heart skip a beat as she watched the sun glint off her diamond-encrusted wedding band. Wow! How life could change in forty-eight hours. She had gone to Vegas to meet her boyfriend, Don, and discuss their relationship problems. Now, she was on the flight home, a married woman – Mrs. Donald Lyons, Don and Beth Lyons, Beth Lyons. It all sounded amazing! The new diamonds, all twenty of them (yes, she had counted) sat in the platinum, channel setting. Don had said that he had chosen an eternity band because he wanted, and needed, her for all eternity. The only problem was that the 10,000 dollar ring (yes, she had looked it up online) could not fill the empty airline seat beside her.

The wedding had been totally unplanned. She and Don lived at opposite ends of the country, and their seven-month relationship was taking a hit due to the distance between them. Beth had been suddenly widowed over a year ago and was busy raising two little boys in Ohio, while Don, a wealthy, Miami bachelor never seemed to have a moment to himself, let alone extra time for her. When they were apart, communication between them was brief, adding to the emotional distance, but when they managed to be together either in Ohio or Miami, life was fabulous. Beth never dreamt that meeting Don on a swingers' cruise the previous fall would have led her to being a married woman once again. Because of the spur of the moment wedding, the bride and the groom were forced to each go their separate ways within a day of the ceremony. Don needed to get back to Miami, while Beth had to figure out how to break the news to family and friends.

The closer the plane came to touching down in her hometown, Kendrick, the more apprehension Beth felt. Few of her friends would be onboard with her marriage. Some just didn't trust Don, while others had issues regarding their relationship. They had lectured Beth time and time again about spending too much time running about the country with her boyfriend while her young sons were pawned off on anyone who would care for them.

Now that they were married, Don and Beth would become a cohesive family, and surely the right thing to do would be to move the boys down to Miami, either into Don's estate or to a newly-purchased home. There were many decisions the two of them had to make and many changes would take place. Marriage presented challenges to all newlyweds, and they were no different. Everything would sort itself out. She and Don would make it happen; and as the wheels screeched on the tarmac, indicating a successful landing, she would soon be explaining the past couple of days and the events that had unfolded.

Beth had flown to Vegas on a Wednesday evening, and now it was Friday afternoon. She had packed for two days and had not thought for a minute about bringing clothes suitable for the Strip, let alone a wedding. Her focus had been on sitting in a hotel room with Don airing her complaints regarding their love affair, listening to his side, of course, and quite frankly, ending the relationship. Between his inability to communicate and his seeming indifference to her sons, as well as the flack her friends heaped on her for neglecting her kids, she was all set to wave the white flag, throw in the towel, and call it quits. She had rationalized, on the flight to Vegas, that it just wasn't worth it. She had been a widow for just over a year. There was no rush to be in such a serious relationship, especially one plagued with so many challenges.

But Don had thought differently. After taking some time alone to think things through, he had decided he didn't want to live without Beth or her kids. He had proposed, and instead of trying to plan a wedding while living thousands of miles apart, Don had convinced her that the quick, easy, and practical way would be to marry while they were together in Las Vegas.

Coming home, she had slightly more belongings than when she had left. As well as her carry-on, she was bringing back a garment bag that protected her beautiful wedding dress and a stunning, albeit pricey, pair of designer wedding shoes. Tucked inside her purse was a small album of wedding pictures and a few dozen wallet-sized ones that she couldn't wait to share.

Yep, she was home. The gray clouds of southeastern Ohio were an unwelcome contrast to the deep blue, cloudless Nevada sky. *Oh well,* she said to herself, *soon the warm sun of Florida will be mine each and every day.* Beth walked to her car and, placing her things in the backseat, made the quick drive to Jack and Cindy Ward's home, dear friends of hers and Richard's for over ten years. Although childless, they were her sons' godparents, and they loved the boys, volunteering to care for them while Beth went to sort things out with Don.

Chapter 2

Pulling up in front of the Ward's house, Beth thought that no one was home. The driveway was empty, and it appeared the house was locked up tight. Beth looked at her watch, and remembering that it was Friday afternoon, realized work and school still held them all captive. She knew someone would have picked up her sons, Max and Matt, from school by now and were probably on their way home. She would give them another ten minutes and then call Cindy.

The phone call was unnecessary. Just as Beth predicted, a car soon pulled into the driveway, and Beth could barely see the heads of two little people in the backseat. Cindy got out of the car and opened the back, driver's side door. The boys had recognized their mother's car and ran at top speed to the vehicle, making it hard for Beth to open her door.

"Hi, Mommy, what did you bring us?" asked Matt, wearing his favorite Batman T-shirt.

"Oh, you little stinkers," laughed Beth. "Is that why you look so excited to see me?"

"Aw, Mom," replied Max, old enough to know what she meant.

"I happen to have a couple of things in my carry-on for two boys – I guess they must be for you two."

"What, Mommy, what?" asked Matt.

Beth reached into the backseat and pulled out a

brightly colored bag. It contained cards, a magic wand, and other paraphernalia necessary for budding magicians. By now, Cindy had the front door unlocked and was waving all three of them into the house. The two boys scampered ahead of Beth and were long gone with their new treasures before she crossed the threshold.

"Hi, Beth, welcome back," said Cindy, as she hugged her friend.

"Thanks, Cindy, how did everything go with the kids?"

"Everything was great, although we really didn't get to spend much time with them. With everyone at school or work all day, it seemed like we only were with the kids a couple of hours after dinner each night."

"Time does fly, doesn't it?" said Beth as she made herself comfortable at the kitchen table.

"Yes, it does. That brings me to something we wanted to ask you," continued Cindy. "Because we didn't see the boys that much, we were wondering if we could keep them for the weekend, if they wanted to stay. We are going to Pittsburgh to stay with my grandparents. There is some cool kid-related stuff going on that we thought the boys would enjoy."

Caught off guard, Beth said, "Have you asked the kids about it?"

"No, we didn't want to mention anything without talking to you first."

"Yes, I guess it would be okay, if they want to."

"Great," said Cindy. "I'll wait until Jackson gets home, and then we can discuss it with them." Changing topics, Cindy had not forgotten Beth's reason for being in Vegas. She didn't want to appear too forward and ask about their relationship status directly, so instead she asked, "How did everything go in Vegas? Did you hit a jackpot?"

"In a way, I did!" exclaimed Beth, dying to break the

news as she held out her left hand, giving Cindy a close up view of her wedding band.

"What the ...?" asked Cindy, who was totally taken off guard, hardly believing what she was seeing. "You got married? Did you leave here with that planned, or what....what the fuck?" She quickly covered her mouth with her hand, realizing the kids were in earshot.

"No, no, not at all. When I left, it was to do just what I told you. My intention was to sit with Don and have a heart to heart. And we did. We both aired all the issues we had and discussed our relationship to death. We came to the conclusion that we loved each other and it was the physical distance between us that was the problem. The best way to overcome it, we figured, was to get married and become a family. I certainly hadn't considered getting married there, without my friends and family, but when Don told me how easy it was to get a license and have a ceremony, I said, why not? We plan on honeymooning later and, in the near future, throwing a celebration here, too."

"Oh, my God, Beth, I never would have guessed. Wait until Jack hears and Jess and everyone else. I can hardly believe it!"

"I know how you feel. If I didn't have this ring on my finger, I might wonder if the whole thing was just a dream."

"So, where is the groom?"

"Back in Miami. We didn't plan any of this, so he hadn't made any arrangements to be away from work. We'll have to figure out when we can get together next."

"Oh, that's sad that you have to be apart already."

"I know, but we've come to terms with it. Before too long, we will be together permanently," said Beth, her eyes shining.

By now, the kids were sitting on the living room carpet examining their junior magicians' kits, totally oblivious to the decision their mom had made that would affect the rest of their lives.

"If you can stay, I'll make a pot of coffee. Oh hell, forget the coffee. I don't know about you, but I need a drink, a stiff one," Cindy said. "And you have no choice but to stay for dinner. I need to hear every last detail, and you have to be here when Jack gets home. He is going to have to hear this from you or he won't believe it," gushed Cindy.

"Well, I guess there is no hurry for me to get home. Sure, I'll stay."

"I just noticed your hair. Look at how long it is, and it's red!"

"I know. Just before the wedding, as a surprise, I had it dyed and extensions put in."

"Okay, just another detail you need to fill me in on," demanded Cindy with a grin. "But don't start now; we have to wait for Jack."

To change the topic, Beth asked how the boys had been in her absence. They had just begun this conversation when Cindy's phone rang. It was Jack informing his wife that he was on his way home.

"Beth is here," Cindy told her husband, "and she is staying for dinner."

"That's great. See you both soon. Bye, ladies," said Jack as he ended the call.

"Jack will be home soon, and I can't wait!" Cindy said smiling.

True to his word, Jack came through the front door less than half an hour later. As he was kicking off his shoes, Matt and Max both went running, with whoops of glee, practically tackling him to the ground. He continued to rough house with them until Cindy came into the room and told everyone to settle down. Then she kissed her husband hello. Their enthusiastic greeting was a sad scenario for Beth. It reminded her of the welcome the boys had often given her late husband, Richard, on his return from work. Immediately, she felt uncomfortable. It was like an out of body experience, watching an interaction between a mom, dad, and their two little boys. But the two little boys were hers, and she was not included in the happy, family portrait.

Jack had taken the time to spend a few minutes looking at the boys' magic kits. Then he entered the kitchen. He was in his mid-thirties. He and Richard had built a solid working relationship as architects that had blossomed into a tight friendship over the years. Jack's hobby was spending time in the gym, and it showed despite the shirt, tie, and suit he wore each day to the office. Walking over to Beth, the two good friends kissed and tightly embraced.

"Hey, Beth, how's it going?" he asked while loosening his purple, black and gray striped tie and unbuttoning the tight, top button of his lavender dress shirt. Jack had always been a good looking guy. With his shaved head and muscular build, he fit the profile of a gym rat, and that's exactly what he was. Working out and weight lifting was his hobby, and it showed deliciously. Jack was the perfect companion for his wife. With no children of their own, they had plenty of time to work out together. Although Cindy didn't weight lift, she was in top physical shape as well. Her lean, muscular body looked great on her 5 foot 10 inch frame that was softened by her very long, thick, gorgeous brown hair. She and Jack would make a perfect couple for the cover of any fitness magazine.

"Hi, Jackson, going great. Thanks for looking after the boys for me," Beth said.

"Those two knuckleheads?" said Jack, affectionately. "We love having them. So, how was Vegas?"

"Oh, you know. Same old, same old. Noisy, dirty, crowded. Such a great place for people-watching though. There are some crazy-assed folks in this world." Beth grinned.

"And a great place for getting married," said Cindy, unable to contain the news any longer.

"What?" said Jack, as he looked quizzically between Beth and his wife.

"It's true," replied Beth as she held out her left hand as proof.

"Beth is going to tell us all the details, right, Beth? Now! Right, Beth?" said Cindy, trying to disguise her demand in the form of a question.

"Okay, okay. You better have a seat, and a drink, Jack," warned Beth as Jack poured Bourbon into a glass, eager to take Beth up on her offer. "When I left here Wednesday night, I really didn't know how this was going to go. I knew I loved Don, but he has always been inattentive to me and the kids when we weren't together, which was most of the time. He was terrible at communicating long distance. I couldn't get used to him not returning my calls or answering my texts, and it felt as though he was indifferent to our relationship. Here is just one example. You both know Tom, from the club. He and I had been intimate many times as swingers. He felt terrible about Richard's death and offered to take the boys and me to his place in Sicily for a vacation. No strings attached, at least that's what he said, but I'll get to that in a minute.

Even when I mentioned the trip to Italy to Don, he

never asked whom I was going with. If the tables had been turned, I would have wanted to know every detail of the itinerary. For me, things came to a head in Italy. Tom explained that his and Rosa's marriage was for convenience only and that Rosa had put a stop to him seeing me. Then we found out she had a boyfriend, and Tom said he loved me. I became very confused. So, to try to sort things out, after I returned home, I demanded Don and I meet to see where our relationship stood. I arrived in Vegas, and he was waiting for me at a bar in Caesar's Palace, as we had planned. I intended to have a good night's sleep and wait until the next morning to have a serious conversation with him, but my issues started to come out while we were in the bar. Basically, I gave him a quick run-down of why I was unhappy. I was very tired by that time and went up to the room to bed. Don said he needed some alone time to think things over, so he went for a long walk. I have no idea what time he came to the room, but when I woke up the next morning, things were different."

"What do you mean, different?" asked Cindy, hanging on every word.

"I feel like I woke up to a whole different Don. He kissed me good morning, and then I went to have a shower. When I came out of the bathroom, there was a dozen, red roses on the table, and room service had just delivered a table for two with a beautiful breakfast. I threw on a robe and sat down to eat. When I took the silver dome off my plate, I saw a jewelry box. Before I could say anything, Don snatched it, got down on one knee and proposed. I said yes, and we toasted our engagement with the mimosas that were on the breakfast table.

"Oh, wow! That's the engagement part, but how did you two decide to take it a step further and get married?"

asked Jack.

"Our first thought was about the wedding. When? Where? How? We both agreed that we didn't want a long engagement, and we didn't want a big wedding. We tossed around the idea of a resort-type wedding in the Caribbean, getting married here in Kendrick, or maybe just heading to Vegas for something short and sweet in the near future. Then it dawned on us that we were already in Vegas. It was possible to get married in a day, so why wait?"

"Did you have a real wedding?" asked Cindy.

"Of course they did. They are married, aren't they?" replied Jack, scolding his wife in fun.

"I know that! But did you have a wedding dress, flowers, or pictures?"

"Yep, all of the above. I think Don wouldn't have cared if we got married in shorts and a tank top, but I insisted that I look like a bride and he look like the groom. We were staying at Caesar's Palace, and the Forum Shops have anything you could want. I didn't want to waste time, so I went to the hotel's concierge and had him narrow down the stores and services that could help me. I knew I wanted to get extensions and the process was lengthy, so I made the earliest appointment possible. While waiting, I went shopping. My dress was my top priority. I was lucky enough to find the perfect dress right off the rack. I have it in the car, and I'll show you some wedding pictures in a few minutes."

"What's it like?" asked Cindy.

"It's cream-colored satin, long, form-fitting with a flare near the bottom that extends to a short, round train. It has a sweetheart neckline, and the bodice is encrusted with crystals as are the medium width straps. But it's the back of the dress that is so amazing. From my shoulders down to my waist is very sheer with the odd crystal here and there just to add some shimmer. Then from one shoulder, hanging down to my waist, then up to the opposite shoulder, is a piece of ivory satin that drapes to a swag. It fit me perfectly with no alterations needed."

"Oh, it sounds so beautiful," said Cindy in awe.

"It really is, Cindy."

"Did you wear a veil?"

"No, I wore a crystal headband with my hair up loosely with tendrils hanging down about my face. I didn't wear any jewelry because of all the lovely beading on my gown. After finding my dress, I still had time before my hair appointment, so I went shoe shopping. I found just what I was looking for at the Christian Louboutin store."

"You mean he has his own store in Vegas?"

"Yes, right in the Forum Shops."

"So, did you have any luck?"

"Too much!" Beth smiled. "It was so hard to choose a pair. I finally narrowed it down to a pair called 'follies lace.' Almost the entire shoe is nude-colored lace with the signature red sole."

"Any flowers?"

"I put Don in charge of his tuxedo and the flowers, and he did a great job. I carried several dozen, petite, blush roses. They were ivory with just a hint of peach at the tips of the petals. Their stems were gathered together with gold satin fabric studded with crystals. Don wore the same rose and embellishment on his black tuxedo lapel. Let me tell you, he looked hot!" reminisced Beth.

As Beth passed around her small wedding photo book, she beamed with pride. It would take an idiot not to see how Beth glowed in each picture standing next to her man. Beth was right. Don did look very handsome in his tux, and Beth was stunning in her gorgeous gown. As

Cindy flipped through the pages, she felt sad that she had been left out of the celebration. She knew a few others would feel the same.

"Obviously, the kids don't know."

"I'll wait until they come home on Sunday, so I can sit them down and quietly explain everything. I need to start preparing them for all the changes that will take place. Eventually, we will move to Florida, but that won't be for a few months, at least. I'll need to sell our house here first. Don and I still need to come to a decision about where in Miami we will live."

"Of course, you will all move to Florida," said Cindy, sounding deflated.

"Yes, we will. I just don't know if we will move into Don's estate or buy a different home. Although his place is spectacular, it's not very homey. I'd like to find something else on the water that is more kid-friendly. We also have to look into some type of school for the boys."

"What do you mean 'some type' of school?" asked Cindy.

"Don says the school system in Miami is not good enough for the kids. He would like to see them in a private school, even a private boarding school, seeing as we can afford it."

"Really, Beth? You would ship your boys off to boarding school?"

"You make it sound as though that would be a bad thing. They would get an education few families could afford."

"Maybe when they are older, but they're just eight and nine years old now. How could you stand not having them with you? And they would be so homesick," said Cindy, looking at Jack pleading for backup.

"Don hasn't raised any kids, so you need to do what is

best for you and the boys – you know them better than anyone. Be careful, and make the right decision," said Jack, agreeing with his wife but trying to be polite.

"Nothing is written in stone. We both have many details to work out," Beth reminded her friends. Eager to change the subject, Beth called both boys into the kitchen and explained that Aunt Cindy and Uncle Jack wanted to take them to Pittsburgh for the weekend. Matt started jumping up and down with excitement while Max, a little more subdued, asked why.

"There is a Lego show in Pittsburgh this weekend, and we know how much you both like Legos," explained Cindy.

"We could also go to the Science Center," added Jack.

"When would we go?" asked Max.

"We would leave tomorrow morning and come home Sunday afternoon. We will sleep at Cindy's grandma's house. You've met them before but you might not remember. What do you think? Would you two like to go?"

"Yes!" yelled Matt.

"Sure," chorused his brother.

"Okay, it's decided then," said Beth.

"How about we order some Chinese food for dinner?" suggested Jack.

"Sounds delicious," answered Beth. And with that, Cindy found the take-out menu, and they ordered dinner. It was fun to sit around the dinner table with friends, and when Beth broke open her fortune cookie, its message alluded to communication, reminding her to call her groom. Jack and Cindy also wanted to talk to Don and offer him their congratulations, but all they could do was leave a voicemail.

Beth helped Cindy clean up after dinner while Jack hung out with the two magicians-in-training. It would soon be time to tuck the boys in for the night, and Beth was looking forward to sleeping in her own bed. It had been a crazy couple of days. She kissed the boys good night, thanked her friends for dinner, and started the drive home. *The house will be quiet without the kids,* thought Beth. *Who am I kidding? It will feel empty.* Suddenly, she felt lonely. No kids, no husband, just an empty house waiting for her.

Maybe she was still on Vegas time, maybe she was too excited to sit still, or maybe she just couldn't wait to share her news, but whatever the reason, she found herself parking in front of Jess and Eric Johnsons' home. Beth hoped they hadn't gone to the club on this Friday evening. Although the lights were on, Beth was unsure who was in the house, so instead of tapping on the door and then walking in, she knocked quietly and remained on the stoop. Happily, Eric answered the door and ushered her in with a hug. Jess appeared from down the hall in her pajamas, her wavy, auburn hair bouncing on her shoulders. She smiled as she saw their visitor. Beth and Richard had been good friends with Jess, Eric, and their son, Ben, for many years. Beth and Jess had gone to the same high school, and they had re-connected when Jess was hired to babysit the Anderson boys after Beth returned to work. Living only a couple of blocks apart meant they saw each other almost daily.

"Hi, you two," started Beth.

"Hey, you're home. Welcome back," said Jess, not knowing what Beth's mood would be.

"Hi, Jess, how did the surgery go?" asked Beth, deliberately skirting the elephant in the room but genuinely concerned, knowing her friend had had minor surgery.

"It went well, thanks. I'm to take it easy for a few days, and those days are almost up. Come Monday, I should be good as new."

"Glad to hear everything is okay," said Beth.

"Well…" urged Jessica as Beth and Eric followed her into the kitchen.

"Well, what?" teased Beth.

"Come on, girlfriend, what the heck happened in Las Vegas?"

"THIS happened in Vegas," admitted Beth as she held out her left hand.

"What the hell?" said Eric, as Jess simply stared at the ring, dumbstruck.

"You got married?" said Eric, stating a fact while asking a question all at the same time.

"Aah, Jess, what's wrong? You have nothing to say."

"Oh, my God, Beth, this is not what I was expecting," said Jess, finally finding her voice after the initial shock began to wear off. She leaned over, and gave her friend a big hug. Eric, too, got to his feet giving Beth a kiss on the cheek. They were more shocked than impressed; but what was done was done.

"I think you need to start at the beginning, like when you stepped off the plane in Vegas. And you better not leave out any of the good stuff," warned Jess.

At that, Eric figured it was his cue to resume watching television. Quite frankly, the wedding details were girl talk. He would leave the two friends to "ooh" and "aah" over the romantic details.

Beth began at the beginning, and after an hour had elapsed, she concluded her tale by showing Jessica the small book of wedding pictures as well as her new hair extensions.

"Let me see that ring again!" commanded Jess.

Slipping it off her finger, Beth offered it to her friend for further inspection.

"This is the most bling on a ring I have ever seen," admired Jess as she slipped it onto her own finger.

"I know," said Beth. "I couldn't help but google it. With that many diamonds in a platinum channel setting, it is worth the price of a small car."

"What is Don's band like?"

"He doesn't have one. This all happened so fast that I didn't have time to buy one. He didn't seem keen on wearing one, but I think the kids and I will pick one out and surprise him with it. I know he doesn't need one, but I would like him to wear it."

"Kind of like marking your territory?" teased Jess.

"Something like that," smiled Beth.

Don looked very hot in his tuxedo, and Beth looked radiant in a gown that looked as though it had been made for her. Once Jess finished ogling the photos, Beth continued with the account of the day's events.

"After the ceremony, we had a lovely dinner at the Rosewood Grille. Don chose the restaurant because it was small, chic, and the food was supposed to be delicious. He had called earlier and set up a, more or less, private table for two. The place was very intimate anyway and, because the staff knew we had just gotten married – I'm sure the tux and wedding dress didn't tip them off at all," smirked Beth, "their service was impeccable, and the bottle of champagne was free!"

"So what did you guys celebrate with?"

"Don had preordered, so we didn't have to bother with menus. It was seamless. We started out with oysters Rockefeller and miniature crab cakes, which were delicious, by the way. The restaurant is known for its fresh lobsters that diners pick out of a tank. We had the staff pick one out for us, and they chose a seven pounder. It was broiled and served with twice-baked potatoes and freshly baked bread. And if that wasn't enough, we had chocolate mousse sprinkled with 23 karat, edible gold for dessert."

"Sounds fantastic!"

"The funny part was when the waiter put a bib on each of us with a tacky picture of a lobster on it. We looked a little strange dressed for the altar with plastic bibs on. Don had the staff take pictures of us with his phone. I knew the bill would be high, and I was right. It came to about 600 dollars, and I wanted to pay for it because Don had taken care of arranging so much of the wedding. But he thought it should be the man's responsibility to foot the bill. After arguing about it for a few minutes, he let me pay, reminding me that we should amalgamate bank accounts anyway: that his money would be my money soon."

"I guess you two have a lot of business issues to take care of now that you are married. You're married! I still can't believe it!" screeched Jess. "What about the boys? What did they say?"

"They're staying with Jack and Cindy until Sunday. They have plans to take them to Pittsburgh. I'll wait until they come home on Sunday to talk to them."

"I think we should throw a party for you guys, like the reception you never had! We could hold it at Club Climax in one of their back rooms. Do you think Don would be able to come?"

"What a great idea. That would be such fun!" said Beth. "With some notice, I think he could organize things and leave for a few days."

"I'm going to call Cindy and a few others and get things organized. You will only have to show up."

"Speaking of the club, I'm at loose ends. With my husband in Miami and my kids in Pittsburgh, I need a diversion. Are you guys going to Climax tomorrow night, by chance?" asked Beth.

"We planned on it. Did you want to join us?"

"I would love to. Hey, Jess, can you keep my marriage to yourself? I want to be able to break the news, so I can see people's reactions."

"Of course, it's your news to tell."

"I feel like I am finally coming down from this high I've been on. I'm beginning to feel tired. I better head for home."

"Have a good night. We will pick you up tomorrow evening."

Beth hugged Jess and Eric as she was leaving. The door latched shut behind her, and Jess and Eric could only stare at each other in bewilderment.

"I did not see that coming," said Jess. "I was preparing myself to console her because of a breakup."

"I didn't know if they would break up, but I certainly didn't think she would come home married. I don't know about Beth, but I think Don is a lucky man."

"No argument there, but I don't have a good feeling about this. Maybe she knows him better than I think she does. It just seemed too rushed. I hope she didn't marry him because she is lonely."

"Come on, Jess. We have to give Beth more credit than that. The stakes are too high because of her kids for her to take such a big step without being sure."

"I wonder how the kids will take the news. I know for sure they barely know him."

"Well, no matter what, we will always be here for those boys," said Eric.

"All we can do at this point is give her the benefit of the doubt. Let's hope she made a smart decision. We have a party to plan!"

"You talk to Jack and Cindy about it, and I'll help wherever you need me."

"Thanks, babe," said Jess, as they both began watching television, each having a hard time concentrating on the screen.

Beth unlocked the door to the dark house, switched on the hall light, then dead-bolted the door behind her. Now that she was alone, she needed to call her groom and let him know her friends' reactions to their news. She was excited about the upcoming wedding reception and anxious to share that news, too. She hadn't yet posted anything about their marriage on social media, but she would broadcast the news, far and wide, after she visited the club.

This time when she called Don, he answered. The two compared their flights home, and Beth told him about the Wards' and the Johnsons' reactions to their news. She also brought up the wedding reception and asked Don to look at his calendar and set aside a few days for celebration and for attending to some business now that they were married. Beth also reminded him that he needed to spend some time with his stepsons. Don promised to give her his available dates in a day or two. After both admitted to being tired, they ended the call.

Chapter 3

Beth awoke early as ever and lay in bed planning her day. Without the kids, the day was hers alone, and the more she thought about it, the more she knew she would spend it doing chores. Cleaning, laundry, and grocery shopping would take up the lion's share of the day. Then she would hit the shower and get ready for the club. Beth wasn't the least bit interested in club sex tonight with her new groom half a country away, but she was excited to tell her friends about her change in marital status. She had no idea how supportive they would be, but if Jess and Cindy were a barometer, other friends would be delighted for her. The only reaction she was a little afraid of was Tom's. He had made it clear how he felt about her despite the fact that his wife had no intention of divorcing him. That was the lynch pin for Beth. She would not be anyone's mistress. Either Tom loved her enough to tackle a complicated and costly divorce so he could marry her or she would not consider developing a relationship with him. He had described at length why he and Rosa would not divorce which, in Beth's eyes, shut down any chance of a future together. She loved him, but he was taken. She knew Tom would be shocked, but he would get over it.

The day progressed, and Beth was pleased with getting her chores completed. She had very much enjoyed the quiet and solitude and felt a little guilty when she didn't feel overjoyed at the prospect of the kids returning home the following day. Maybe she was dreading telling them about their new step-dad. It wasn't just that another parent was joining the family, but soon everything they knew would change: their address, school, activities and friends. She was somewhat apprehensive to hear their reactions.

Dressed and waiting in the den, Beth heard the Johnsons' SUV. Switching off the light, she made her way to the door picking up the liquor bag and her coat before stepping outside. On the way to the club, Jess shared some news regarding the upcoming party. She and Cindy had put their heads together and had made some lists. Now, all they needed from Beth and Don was the date. Beth had played phone tag with Don all day, and figured she may as well try again while sitting in the backseat.

"Hi, babe," said Beth as Don picked up the call.

"How's my wife?"

"Your wife is great. I'm here with Jess and Eric. We are on our way to the club, and Jess and Cindy need a date for our party. They would like to book the venue tonight while we are there."

"Just a minute. Let me look at my calendar." After a few seconds, he offered, "How about three weeks from now?"

"As long as we can book a party room at the club for that weekend, you're on!"

"Well, let me know how that works out, and you have fun tonight. Don't do anything I wouldn't do," instructed Don, knowing full well Beth wouldn't do half the things he would do! The call ended, and they had chosen a date. Jess said she would check with Jezzy, the club's owner, later that evening.

Beth had decided not to bring up her marriage but not

to hide it either. She knew her ring would give it away, and if anyone mentioned it or asked, she would be happy to relay the details. The interaction with Kristie, at the podium, elicited no reaction. The brief time they spent handing over their coats did not allow Kristie an opportunity to notice the bling on Beth's left hand. *Surely, she would hear about it later*, Beth mused. The next stop was routinely the bar. Here, there was a greater chance for the news to be revealed. At this time of the evening, it would be crowded with patrons seeking pre-dinner libation. And there was eagle-eyed Randy. His undercover police training had honed his ability to notice details, and Beth knew her ring was a little bit more than a detail!

Beth looked over at Jess as they wormed their way through the crowd to the marble-topped bar. Beth could tell it was killing her friend not to be able to spread the news. If truth be told, it was eating at Beth, too. She hoped someone would notice soon, so she could let the cat out of the bag. Randy was the first person to notice with a little help from Beth. As Randy set down the cocktail in front of her, she made sure to reach for it with her left hand. He would have had to be nearly blind not to pick up on the glint produced by the bright pot lights shining down from the bar's ceiling.

"Oh, my God, darlin', what is that gorgeous piece of jewelry on your finger?" said Randy in his soothing Southern drawl.

"Oh, this old thing?" replied Beth. "It's just a wedding band, that's all," she said, demurely.

"Does it mean what I think it means?"

"As far as I know, a wedding ring only means one thing – marriage."

"Did you get married, Beth?" He raised his eyebrows.

"Yes, I did. Don and I tied the knot in Vegas a couple

of days ago." Unlike his usual calm self, Randy had lost his composure and was nearly speechless. He stumbled over a word or two and then offered his congratulations to the bride with a kiss on her cheek.

"And where is the lucky bridegroom?" asked Randy. "I'd like to shake his hand."

"Unfortunately, he had to return to Miami. The wedding wasn't exactly planned, so he hadn't made any arrangements work-wise."

"Oh, I'm sorry you didn't get a honeymoon. I want to hear more, but you'll have to excuse me, darlin'. The drink orders are piling up."

"I'll give you all the details later."

Several members had overheard bits and pieces of their conversation and had gathered closer to Beth to see the ring and offer their congratulations. Jessica delighted in offering details of the nuptials whenever she could get the chance, indicating to all that she had the honor of knowing before nearly anyone else.

As people were being seated for dinner, the threesome took their places at a table. That didn't stop the admirers from taking a closer look at Beth's finger. Just as dinner was beginning, Tom and Rosa rushed in. Rosa was quick to steer them to a table nowhere near Beth and her friends. It was impossible for Tom not to notice the small crowd that had gathered around Beth. *What could be going on?* Tom wondered to himself. Rosa noticed it, too, and politely asked their table mates.

"I heard someone over there was recently married – I can't tell you her name as I don't know the woman." As far as Tom could see, those sitting at the table in question were all couples he recognized. The only single woman was Beth. And that's when it hit him. *It couldn't be Beth who had married,* he reasoned to himself, knowing he was really pleading for it not to be true. *No, it couldn't be.*

The knowledge of his wife's boyfriend had changed many things for Tom. There had been few remaining feelings between the two of them for some time, but they had agreed to stay together for family and to avoid a long, complicated divorce. At one time, Tom had wanted to stay married due to an expensive divorce settlement, not to mention the complexities that would arise during their divorce. But after finding out about his wife's infidelity, he no longer cared about the money. He loved Beth and had decided that life was too short not to be with her. He had been busy getting his financial ducks and personal issues in a row before he would tell Beth his intention to divorce Rosa. He knew that even after his divorce, there would be things to overcome and one of those would be that asshole boyfriend of hers, Don. He appeared to be nothing more than a pain in the ass. Tom had dealt with losers like him before, but if the boyfriend might now be the husband, that was a bigger issue.

Beth had revealed her true feelings for Tom while in Italy. She had also stated she would never be his mistress. If he couldn't divorce Rosa, she wasn't interested in a relationship with him. Tom wondered if Beth had married because she thought her relationship with him was a dead end.

Rosa heard the speculation at the same time her husband did, and her reaction was vastly different. Looking over at the table, she was quite sure the blushing bride was Beth. Her gut told her that her little talk with Don at the airport in NYC had something to do with the quick marriage. It had been pure luck that Don and Rosa had ended up at the airport at the same time when Beth and Don had coincidentally gone to New York the same weekend Tom and Rosa had. She had not hesitated to make sure Don knew that Tom had a very strong interest in Beth and had for some time. After all, once a fellow knows other men are interested in his girl, it's only natural that he makes sure they can't have her.

Looking over and seeing the troubled look on Tom's face made Rosa's day. She was having a hell of a good time. Tom's face was a mixture of uncertainty, fear, disbelief and shock mixed with just a hint of anger. God, it was glorious. She relished the turmoil she knew he was feeling.

Tom desperately wanted to march over to Beth and find out if the rumors he had heard were true. But for once in his life, he didn't have the nerve. No, he couldn't confront her about this – at least not in public. He knew his buddy Randy would know the details by now. He would visit the bar for some information and a much needed drink.

"What? Beth is married?" asked Rosa, feigning disbelief as she failed to restrain herself from egging Tom on.

"I don't know. I guess we'll find out later," answered Tom, calmly, not wanting to show his wife that he was upset. As hard as he tried, Tom could not become immersed in his dinner companions' conversations, nor could he refrain from looking over at Beth every five seconds. He couldn't head to the bar yet; that would be too obvious to everyone, especially Rosa. He would wait until after dessert if this fucking, tedious meal would ever end.

Had Beth noticed Tom and Rosa come into the dining room, she would have been stoked. There was no one she wanted to show off her new ring, new name, and new marital status to more than Tom. He could keep all his fucking money and his wife!

Finally, the servers were clearing away the dishes, and

many of the diners were leaving their tables to get a drink, head to the dance floor, or change into appropriate club clothing. Word of Beth's ring had somehow spread during dinner, and once again, there were several women salivating over her out-stretched hand. Rosa had left for the ladies' room, giving Tom an opportunity to speak to Randy.

Randy finished pouring several martinis. Then he moved over to where Tom stood and began reaching for Tom's stock bottle of Scotch.

"Hey Randy, what's all the commotion over Beth tonight?" asked Tom, trying to sound nonchalant.

"Thought you would have heard by now. She up and got married a couple of days ago, so she says."

"What the hell! You think you know someone..." Tom's voice trailed off as Randy confirmed his fear.

"I'm as sorry as you are. We both had reservations about Don."

"Whether he's married to Beth or not, I know there is something off about that guy."

"If it's any help, I overheard Jess talking about having a reception here in a private dining room in the near future. I presume the groom will be in attendance."

"I would enjoy tangling with him again," said Tom, remembering his last communication with Don. *Might be able to learn more about the snake straight from his own mouth. But in the meantime, I had better put on a happy face and go congratulate the bride.*

"Thanks, Randy. I see my wife over there already examining Beth's hand. Guess I should join her."

"Good luck, brother. I'll fix you a double," offered Randy.

As Randy put the glass down on the bar, it was instantly retrieved by Tom, who in one, quick swig downed the entire glass of smooth, expensive liquor. Replacing the empty glass on the bar top, he took a deep breath and turned toward Beth and his wife.

"Good evening, ladies," said Tom to the small group. "I hear congratulations are in order."

"Our little Beth, here, tells us she got married to Don Lyons a couple of days ago," replied Rosa, smirking as the words left her mouth.

"That's what I hear. It's all the buzz tonight. Well, Beth, congratulations. I hope you and Don will be very happy," said Tom as he took a step forward planting a kiss on her left cheek. "If you ladies will excuse me."

As Tom moved toward the bar, Rosa joined him. "Well, good for Beth," said Rosa. "It's nice she has found love after what she has been through."

"Yes, it sure is," replied Tom, knowing his comment carried as much heartfelt sentiment as his wife's.

Everyone interested in Beth's news had eventually connected with her and then went the way of the dance floor or the playrooms. Beth was not the least bit interested in having sex with anyone and was using the evening as a social occasion only. Coming out of the ladies' room, she could see that the bar was deserted, and Randy was washing up a stack of dirty glasses. Just as she walked toward him, she was interrupted by Jess.

"I called Cindy, and we made some plans. It's all taken care of. I talked to Jezzy and tentatively reserved three weeks from tonight for the reception."

"Thanks, Jess. I'll try to get a hold of Don to confirm before I leave the club, but if I can't, I'll keep trying once I'm home."

"This is going to be so much fun!" giggled Jess.

Jessica made her way down the hall to find her husband while Beth continued on to the bar. Sitting down on a bar chair, Beth took her phone from her purse and called Don. As usual, it went to voicemail. Leaving a message, she ended the call and placed her phone on the bar top as Randy walked toward her.

"Hey, sweet stuff," said Randy, affectionately, "you sure are the topic of conversation tonight."

"I know. It's been a whirlwind couple of days."

"Laura's not here tonight, but when I tell her about you gettin' hitched, she is going to hit me up for all the details. So now that I have you all to myself, darlin', let's hear everything from top to bottom," urged Randy. He wasn't as interested in the details for Laura as he was for future activities, namely helping Tom investigate the bridegroom.

Beth was enjoying nothing more than recapping all that had happened to her and Don in Vegas and the history between them that had acted as the catalyst leading to the hasty marriage. She concluded by telling Randy that the celebration would end with the reception at Club Climax which her friends were currently planning.

Most everyone knew that Randy was a police detective, originally from South Carolina, who was very adept at stepping out of his professional persona to become just a good ole boy at the club. Beth had no idea that Randy was subtly directing the conversation, so he could glean as much helpful information about Don as possible.

He ended his visit with Beth by saying, "I hope everything turns out alright for you two."

After a few cocktails with Randy, it was still too early to expect her friends to want to go home, so she ordered one more from the bar to take outside to the fire pit. With only one young couple enjoying the flames and each other, there were plenty of seats for Beth to choose from.

The couple paused their foreplay as they welcomed Beth. Noting Beth appeared to be alone, they looked at each other, shrugged, and then asked if she would like to join them. Beth smiled but politely declined. She could not resist telling them about her recent marriage and missing husband. After several more minutes of fondling, the couple left the fire, laughing all the way to a playroom.

The patio was quiet. Although the fire crackled in the pit, the black, resin wicker chairs remained empty. All of a sudden, Beth began to feel lonely and sorry for herself. It would help if Don would answer his phone. They had discussed their communication, or lack thereof, at length, and she thought she had gotten through to him. But tonight, she wasn't so sure, as her eyes welled up with tears. Taking a deep breath, she smiled to herself. *I'm being unrealistic. No one is available to pick up their phone every minute of every day.* She needed patience and was hopeful they would talk before the night was over.

Tom's night had been far from enjoyable. Beth's news had slapped him across the face, and its sting had been with him all evening. Tom and Rosa, no longer intimate, had gone their separate ways early in the evening. Rosa had visited with many of her friends, caring only to be sexually active with her boyfriend, Sam, who was not a swinger. Tom, on the other hand, had quickly looked for a sex partner – someone on whom to take out his frustrations. He was well-known at the club, and seldom did a woman turn down the sensuous, gentle, thoughtful caresses of his fornicating. The lucky lady, Lydia, had hastily joined him in a playroom where he closed both the door and the blinds, signaling he wanted complete privacy.

"Take off your clothes," demanded Tom.

"Sure Tom," said Lydia, somewhat hesitantly. Tom

yanked at the buttons on his shirt and hastily threw it along with his shoes, trousers, socks and underwear. He waited for Lydia to undress to her lace bra and panties. Tom unceremoniously nudged her back onto the bed. Forcing his knee between her legs, he leaned over her and shoved his tongue into her mouth. Lydia attempted to slow down his kisses and tongue thrusts with gentle kisses in return. Tom would not have it. He continued exploring her mouth with his probing tongue while he reached between Lydia's legs and, pulling aside the crotch of her panties, thrust his sizable cock deep into her pussy.

Lydia gasped at the quick penetration- uncomfortable due to lack of lubrication. Tom rested his full weight on Lydia, who was as petite as Beth. She, too, had full breasts that were still encumbered by her bra. Tom wasn't interested in sucking her nipples or giving her any pleasure. He closed his eyes and fucked her, pretending it was Beth. Wanting to feel Beth under him, wanting her arms and legs wrapped around him. He thrust his cock and mouth into Lydia again and again until he reached his peak and shot his load into her. He was still ejaculating when he pulled out and flopped onto his back next to her. Without a word, he immediately sat up and reached for his clothing.

Lydia, dumbfounded by Tom's treatment, lay in complete silence waiting for Tom to leave. This was not the Tom whom Lydia knew – that man was nowhere to be seen. There had been nothing sensuous about his moves, nothing generous about his foreplay, and definitely nothing gentle about his entry or thrusting. It had been selfishly all about him, and even after it was over, he had quickly left the bathroom making a beeline to the bar. The quick tryst had left him feeling no better, with anger still trapped in his gut. He knew alcohol wasn't the answer either yet ordered a double Scotch from Randy, hoping he could soon convince his wife it was time to go home.

Beth had enjoyed a pleasant evening basking in the limelight. She had had a great time sharing her news and showing off her new jewelry. But now, she was tired and wanted to find Eric and Jess with the hopes of going home. She made her way back inside the club and headed down the halls looking into the various playrooms but did not find her friends. The fire had been warm, and Beth made her way back out to the patio. As she opened the outside door, the fire's glow made Tom's face easily recognizable as he sat alone. Tom looked up from the flames as soon as he saw the light from the door. "Hey, come on over and sit down," he urged.

"Actually, Tom, I was looking for Jess and Eric."

"Last I saw them, they were busy in the crimson playroom. You may as well have a seat," he said, patting the chair next to him. Not particularly anxious to hear what he had to say, but having no excuse not to join him, Beth took a seat.

"Okay, Tom, what's on your mind?" Some kind of snort came out of his mouth ending in a sneer. Beth didn't like where this was heading.

"The elephant in the room, that's all, Beth."

"I know it's a surprise for everyone."

"A surprise?" said Tom, "A surprise? I made an effort to make sure you were forewarned about Don. I really figured you were smarter than this. In fact, as I recall, you, yourself, told me you had no intention of moving quickly with him or making decisions that could jeopardize your family – yet look at your left hand," he went on as he reached for her hand as he spoke.

"I'm sorry that you're upset, Tom, but I've done what I

felt was right."

"You felt, but you didn't think. It's your life Beth, but I hope there will be someone there to pick up the pieces when all this comes crashing down around you. Oh, and you should find a pediatric therapist because your kids are going to need one." With that, Tom threw the stub of his cigar into the fire pit and left Beth alone in the glow of the flames. Tom's words were hard to hear. She had hoped he would be as gracious to her in private as he had been in public, earlier in the evening. It was not surprising that he had felt the need to lecture her, and now that it was over, she hoped all negativity was behind her. Beth remained alone on the patio. The fire was comforting as she once again called Don. She felt wounded, and she knew hearing his voice would set things right.

"Damn it," said Beth out loud when no one picked up and voicemail was her only option. She ended the call with the push of a button, and after several more minutes of solitude, decided to take a walk past the playrooms to the club's entry, hoping to find Eric and Jess waiting for her.

"Hi, doll, how are you?" gushed Kristie.

"I'm doing alright. I miss Don, of course, but thought I could use some distraction," explained Beth.

"Let me see!" squealed Kristie as she grabbed Beth's left hand. "It's gorgeous!"

"Thank you! I guess everyone here knows, then?" asked Beth.

"Yep! And we are all very happy for you Beth. Will you be participating tonight?"

"No, Don and I are going to set down some new rules now that we are married. I'll be observing only."

"Okay, honey. I brought a friend tonight. Maybe you

can watch us – we would love it. I'm nearly done with check-in," said Kristie as she glanced at her watch. "We'll be in the Zebra Room."

"Sounds good. I'll catch you later. I need a drink from Randy!"

"See ya, Beth," said Kristie with a wink to her friend, as she turned to the two couples who had just walked in.

Beth made a beeline to the familiar bar and even more familiar bartender. Not having spotted her friends, Beth decided she might as well spend time with Kristie and her partner.

"Hi, Randy," smiled Beth as she climbed the steps to the bar.

"Want a Cosmo?"

"Love one, please."

"I almost didn't recognize you with all that hair," said Randy as he handed Beth her drink.

"Well, Don likes redheads, and I thought I was due for a change."

"Has Tom seen it yet?" asked Randy.

"You are direct, aren't you, Randy?" laughed Beth.

"Sorry, Beth."

Beth didn't answer, but smiled, took a sip of her drink and then began walking back to Kristie's playroom. Kristie chose the room with the hanging sex swing. It also housed a king bed centered in the room adorned with nothing more than crisp white sheets. Closing the door behind the threesome, Beth also shut the blinds to the viewing window. She took a seat on the bed and kicked off her shoes, so her screaming feet could breathe a little.

Kristie was clad in a see-through negligee and a pink thong standing next to a matching Malibu Barbie.

"Beth, meet my friend Robin."

Beth clasped Robin's hand. She gave Beth a firm

squeeze along with her shake.

"Nice to meet you, Robin," said Beth as she admiringly took all of Robin in. Robin stood equally as tall as Kristie, with long, straight dirty blonde hair cut in the same fashion as Kristie's including bangs straight across her forehead. She appeared to love the color pink as did Kristie, wearing it both on her lips, and the tight Lycra tube-top dress, which barely covered her full breasts, ass, and crotch. She was just as tanned as Kristie, and both girls wore similar silver, strappy stiletto shoes allowing them to tower over Beth.

"Are you ready for a little voyeurism, Beth?" Kristie asked sweetly.

"I've got nothing else planned, so sure!"

Robin began kissing Kristie gently at first, then with fervor as Kristie plunged her tongue into Robin's mouth. Their tongues fought for maximum occupancy as their hands ran up and down each other's bodies. Kristie grasped the back of Robin's dress and finding the zipper, yanked it down, freeing her from her clothing. She wore nothing beneath, and her beautiful, hairless body was equally as stunning as Kristie's. She stepped out of her dress and pulled off her shoes. Now kneeling, Robin wrapped her long fingers around each of Kristie's thighs and buried her face in between her legs. She grabbed Kristie's thong and pulled it down to the floor around her ankles. Kristie took a wider stance, kicking her miniature piece of fabric aside.

Robin stuck out her tongue and began licking Kristie between her pink inner pussy lips. She found her cunt hole and slipped her tongue in as deeply as she could.

"Mmm," replied Kristie as she backed away and sat her beautiful round ass into the swing. With Robin's help, she slipped her feet through the foot harness and spread her legs wide apart. Kristie hung onto the handcuffs but did not strap her hands within. Robin dove her face between Kristie's legs once again and worked her pussy over like Beth had never seen a woman do before. She never came up for air!

"Beth, can you grab the dildo out of my bag over there?" asked Robin.

"You bet," said Beth as she pulled out an impressive, life-like, skin-toned dildo with visible veins and a circumcised head.

Robin shoved it into her own mouth for lubrication. Then she touched Kristie's vaginal opening with it. She refrained from inserting, instead continuing to lick Kristie's quivering clit. Robin moved up to Kristie's tits for a brief minute to suckle her rosy nipples.

"Fuck me," moaned Kristie.

Robin starting turning and advancing the huge dildo inside Kristie's tight twat, inch by inch until it was almost out of sight. Then, pushing the swing away from her, but still holding onto the fake cock, she plunged it inside with every swing toward her and pulled out every time Robin pushed the swing backward. Kristie caught the rhythm, and like a child, she began to swing herself toward and then away from Robin and her pleasurable cock, allowing Robin to concentrate on the job at hand. In and out, Beth watched the disappearing act made possible by Robin, the magician.

Kristie's moans were getting louder, when she said, "Lick my clit, so I can cum."

Robin grabbed the left cable that suspended the swing from the ceiling, stilling the movement of the chair. Keeping the dildo deep within Kristie' pussy, she used her right hand to spread Kristie, revealing her reddened clit. Robin ran her wet tongue back and forth, then in circles over it until she felt Kristie arch her back and buck toward her mouth.

"Ahh, oh my God, oh my God," repeated Kristie. Robin kept her tongue lightly on her clit – lightly flicking it with her tongue as she pulled out the dildo and threw it to the floor. She moved her tongue inside Kristie's snatch and caught the flowing juices as she felt the walls clamp down on her tongue.

"That felt great. Thank you," said a near breathless Kristie.

"You're welcome, baby," Robin replied as she stood upright to kiss Kristie's still eager mouth.

"Your turn. How do you want it?" asked Kristie with a sly smile playing on her mouth.

"In the ass, of course," laughed Robin.

Never a dull moment when Kristie's involved, thought Beth. *Here we go!*

Chapter 4

Beth began to stir, then opened her eyes. The bedside clock said it was 6:30. Despite the fact that she had only been in bed for five hours, and there were no kids in the house, she knew rolling over and trying to sleep more would be futile. Sitting up and flinging back the covers, she swung her legs over the side of the bed and remained seated as she let out a stretch and a noisy yawn. The hardwood felt cool beneath her feet compared to the cozy area rug that surrounded the bed. After using the bathroom and washing her hands, she took the phone from the bedside table and made her way to the kitchen. Her iPad lay on the counter with its umbilical cord feeding it the necessary charge. Uncoupling it, she set both devices on the kitchen table in front of her.

Excited, she decided to spread the word. Taking a picture of her wedding ring, she uploaded it as her new Facebook profile picture. In case that wasn't clear enough, she decided to upload one of their wedding pictures as well. Besides the small photo album, the photographer had given them several dozen, wallet-sized pictures of the two of them. He suggested they could be given out in announcements or thank-you cards. Laying one on the table, Beth snapped a picture of it, uploading it to her timeline. The first post about it would be hers as she explained what it represented. Glancing at her phone, she had the urge to call Don. Even though it was Sunday, she knew the longer she waited to place the call, the less chance she had of connecting with him. It was only 6:45. She'd give him another hour. She had plenty of social media to catch up on. It was amazing how much had been placed on the Internet since before she had gone to Las Vegas. While sipping her coffee, she scrolled through Facebook and caught up on her Scrabble games.

With the better part of an hour gone, she dialed the phone, convinced Don wouldn't be off and running yet. Sure enough, he answered after the second ring.

"Hello, babe, how is my wife?" The word sent shivers down Beth's spine and put a huge grin on her face.

"Hi, sweetheart, I'm good, except I miss you like crazy."

"I know. Me, too. How was the club last night?"

"For the most part, it was great. I had fun telling everyone we got married and showing them our wedding pictures and my ring. Everyone was very excited for us except Tom, of course. He thinks I'm crazy."

"Fuck him! He's just jealous that I married the most beautiful lady on the planet," said Don.

"I know, right?" agreed Beth smugly.

"Did you get busy at the club?"

"No! Not without you! No interest in hooking up with anyone with you clear across the country, but I'm hoping that will change."

"The hooking up part or me across the country?" asked Don, slyly.

"You being across the country. I know that will change, at least temporarily, when you come here for the wedding reception."

"That's very nice of them to organize a party for us," said Don, not really excited to make another trip to Snoresville. The sooner he could get Beth to Florida and lessen her connection to Ohio, the better. Then, maybe, he could stop having to make the expensive and time-consuming trip north. "Did you see any memorable hookups last night?"

"I watched a creative couple – wishing you were here, so we could have joined in."

"Oh, really, and just what would you have done to me?" asked Don, with a grin.

"No, babe, it's what you would have done to me."

"Do you have your webcam hooked up?"

"Sure, why?"

"We are going to have a little Internet sex, wifey."

"I've never done this before. Can you give me a few minutes to get ready? Then you can lead the way!"

Beth decided she needed to maintain intimacy with Don. Long-distance relationships were difficult, and although she felt a little sheepish about Internet sex, she agreed to give it a try.

Beth had showered earlier and dried her hair. She ran to the bathroom and began applying heavier makeup than her usual daytime look. With smoky eye shadow and eyeliner, Beth finished her seductress look with a pair of false eyelashes. The final touch – a pouty red mouth that complemented her new long, wavy red hair.

She went into her closet and searched through the row of sexy lingerie that was carefully hung on silk fabric clothing hangers. Beth pushed through each piece until she came to the Guia la Bruna negligee with matching side-tied thong panties that Tom had bought her when they were in Italy. That trip seemed like a lifetime ago, she thought wistfully.

Taking the nightie and matching panties, she gently placed them on the bed. She stripped off her yoga pants and tank top and slipped into her outfit. Going to the lingerie drawer of her dresser, she pulled out white, lace-topped thigh-high stockings. After putting them on, she went back into the closet and slid her feet into five-inch stiletto heels to complete her ensemble.

Beth looked at her reflection in the full-length mirror that was hung on the back of her closet door. She had to admit that she looked quite tempting! She could hardly wait for Don's reaction. After fluffing the pillows on her bed, she opened her nightstand drawer and removed her vibrator and lubricant. She turned on her laptop, which she had brought upstairs earlier that morning, connected to the Internet, and found Don waiting for her.

"Hi, babe! You look ravishing this morning!"

"You haven't seen all of me yet," teased Beth.

"Show me," Don said huskily.

Beth positioned her laptop on the corner of her bed so that it was propped on top of several pillows.

"How's that?"

"Wow! I can see all of you. And wow again! You look gorgeous. I love the hair!"

The hair, thought Beth. *I spent all that damn time on makeup, false lashes, thigh highs and heels, and it's my hair he focuses on.*

"Okay, let me see you," Beth said, ignoring his hair comment.

Don positioned his laptop on the end of his bed as well. He was buck naked, wearing only his smile and semi-hard on.

"Cheese!" exclaimed Don.

Beth thought to herself, men have it so easy. No makeup or lingerie....

"Hey – where are you, Don?"

"I'm in bed," replied Don.

"You're not in your master bedroom, baby."

"What? Oh, yeah," scrambled Don. "Uh, I had work to do in my guest house. Does this twin bed bother you, ha ha?"

"No, it just threw me off. I knew that crappy little bed wasn't yours. And that gorgeous black-and-white canvas of Hilton Head Beach was missing above the headboard!"

"Very astute," Don said flatly. "Enough talk, baby," said Don, wanting to get off the current subject.

Taking her cue, Beth slid down the ribbon straps of her negligee and untied the ribbon of the rose-hued bodice, freeing her breasts from the double layers of sheer fabric. She lightly stroked her breasts with her fingertips in a circular pattern until she couldn't resist stimulating her nipples. Semi-erect from excitement, her nips did not need much attention before they became perky and throbbing. She pinched them and rolled them watching for Don's reaction.

Don was stroking his penis and cupping his balls, never taking his eyes off his computer screen. "Yeah, baby," he encouraged.

Beth pulled the hem of her nightie up to just beneath her breasts, exposing her abdomen and thong. She ran her fingers of her right hand up and down her belly while her left hand committed to its job on her breasts.

She dipped her fingers underneath the edge of the top of her thong, out of view.

"Mmm," Beth said for Don's benefit.

She kept her fingers out of sight, stroking up and down underneath the light fabric of her thong. She slowly raised and lowered her pelvis and moved her left hand to help with her right.

"Lose the thong, Beth," commanded Don.

Following Don's order, Beth untied the ribbons holding her thong together. Exposing her pussy to the webcam, she bent her knees and spread her legs for Don. Grabbing the lubricant, she squirted it liberally between her lips as well as the vibrator tip. She spread her pussy lips with a V made by the first two fingers of her left hand. With two fingers of her right hand, she slowly slid her fingertips up and down over her clitoral hood, causing an immediate engorgement of the erectile tissue.

Don groaned and stroked his cock's full length firmly, imagining himself plunging deeply into Beth. He wrapped his hand tighter but kept his rhythm slow, not wanting to cum yet.

Beth watched Don masturbate, completely turned on by him and the sensations within her own body.

Working her clit more vigorously, Beth knew she was going to cum quickly. Her right hand found the vibrator lying beside her, and turning the end to the on position, she heard the familiar hum of the fastest speed.

Using her left hand again, she spread her lips exposing her now juicy vaginal opening. She teased Don by poising the tip of the vibrator at the opening but not inserting it.

"I'm going to pretend you're fucking me, okay?"

Don couldn't answer, but he kept his eyes locked on Beth's every movement.

Beth slowly slid the vibrator into her pussy until the length of it had disappeared. She arched her back and began fucking herself with the vibrator in long, deep strokes. She rocked her pelvis up and down to meet her own rhythm. Her left hand reached up and tweaked her nipples once again.

"Oh yeah – fuck my pussy, Don. Fuck it hard!" yelled Beth.

Don pumped his swollen rod vigorously, almost feeling Beth's pussy walls clamped around his cock meat.

Beth worked the vibrator against her G-spot causing

herself to moan. "Oh, yeah, Don. Right there – right there. Faster, harder," she yelled as she assaulted her cunt at a feverish rhythm.

"I'm cuming!" yelled Don.

"Aah, aah, me too, baby!" yelled Beth as she felt her vaginal walls rhythmically tighten against the now dormant vibrator lying still within her.

"Oh, my God, that felt great," Beth said between deep breaths.

"Damn right," said Don. "You are one hot piece of ass, baby."

"I miss you, Don. I want the next time to be real between us."

"It will be, Beth. I'll see you soon."

"I hope so," said Beth.

"Hey, I got to get back to work, baby."

"I know. I love you, Don."

"I love you, too. Have a good day," said Don as he reached to disconnect his Skype.

It started a whole new trend between them. The more online sex they had, the more Beth wanted. It seemed naughty, like she was watching someone when she shouldn't have. Being a voyeur was fun.

Jack brought the kids back on Sunday afternoon, as promised. They both bounded into the house full of excitement. The weekend had been a great success, and each had a new Lego set to boot. Beth sat down on Max's bedroom floor and built Legos with the boys. Once they had calmed down, it became the perfect time to talk to them about the recent changes.

"Hey, guys, Mommy has some things to talk to you about."

"What?" said Max without stopping his building.

"Well, you know last week when I went away for a few days, and you stayed with Aunt Cindy?"

"Yep."

"I went to talk with Don about how we were getting along, and we decided to get married. And we did," explained Beth, all smiles.

"You mean you got married?" said Matt. "Did you marry Tom?"

"No, silly," said Beth, caught off guard. "Tom is just Mommy's friend. Don is now my husband and your new daddy!"

"But I want Tom to be our new daddy. I like Tom best," whined Matt.

"To marry someone, you have to love them. Mommy doesn't love Tom. Mommy loves Don, and now he loves us. You guys know that Don lives across the country in Florida. Remember we talked about his big house with the swimming pool, his boat, and fishing?" By now, both boys had quit playing and were paying attention. "Once school is over and it's summer, we are going to move to Florida to live with Don. You guys can swim every day, go fishing, and you will go to a new school."

"Will Ben be able to play with us still?" asked Matt.

"Not every day. But we will buy a new house with enough bedrooms so he can come and stay with us any time he comes for a visit." With this new information kicking in and beginning to be understood, Max weighed in. "You mean we would move to Florida forever?" Noticing tears in Max's eyes, Beth reached out to hug him, "Yes, but we can fly back here to see our friends whenever we want. No more cold and snow. We can go to the beach every day. I know it will be a big change, but you two will make lots of new friends, and so will Mommy."

"When, Mommy?"

"Not right away. First, we have to sell our house and find a new one in Florida. But we will take our time. You have lots of days left to play with Ben. Don't worry." The boys seemed to ponder what she had said, and as long as their lives wouldn't change tomorrow, they decided to settle back into the task at hand of building with their blocks. "I'm going to start making dinner," said Beth, as she got up from the floor. Although breaking the news had gone reasonably well, Matt's outburst about Tom had been unexpected. It was obvious her sons had not bonded with Don, and they desperately needed to spend time together. *I guess that will come in time*, thought Beth. *Patience*, she reminded herself. *They had a whole lifetime ahead of them.*

Beth began defrosting meat, and while she waited for the microwave to beep, she gave Don a call. Surprisingly, he answered his phone promptly, once again. "Hey, you are quick to answer my call for the second time today."

"The last time I heard from you, I ended up having a pretty good time," reminded Don of their online sex only several hours ago.

"Oh, and you are hoping for an encore?" asked Beth.

"Anytime, anywhere," assured Don.

"Sorry, babe not this time. The boys are home. Actually, that's what I called about. I broke the news to them about the wedding. That led to reminding them about moving to Florida."

"How did that go?"

"Okay, I think. Of course, they're worried about leaving their friends. But I assured them Ben can come and visit and that they will make new friends in Florida."

"Have you thought about selling your house?"

"I think I should contact a realtor soon. I have no idea

how long it may take to sell."

"You said you wouldn't move until the school year is finished. When is that?"

"They will be finished after the first week of June. Have you begun looking for a new place for us?"

"No, other than thinking about getting the estate ready to sell, I have no idea what is on the market now."

"Can you get a realtor and start looking? Time goes by so fast."

"I'm so busy with work right now, there is no way I can spare the time to take on house-hunting," replied Don in a tone that suggested irritation and an unwillingness to negotiate his house-hunting decision at the moment. The abrupt change in attitude left Beth at a loss for words.

After several awkwardly silent seconds, she replied, "Well, you are the one there. I can look on the Internet and see what is available, but it's not like I'm in a position to go looking at houses."

"I'm not able to spend days touring around Miami either."

"I guess we don't have to go house-hunting tomorrow, but we need to make some plans to get together and see what's out there before too long," said Beth, sensibly.

"I'm sorry, Beth, but I have to go. We can discuss this at another time." And before she could get two more words out, Don had already hung up.

Don was frustrated by his latest business dealing. He needed to make some personnel changes ASAP. If not, heads would roll – including his own. He needed Beth, damn it, but he wouldn't be going to Kendrick for almost another month. Slipping his hand between the mattress and box spring of the bed, he found what he was looking for – a DVD. He popped it into his laptop and placed it beside him on the bed. He tapped the play button, and then he relaxed back into the pillows. Don didn't often watch porn – he was too busy with work – and was seldom short of sex partners. But tonight, he had a special appetite that needed to be satisfied.

Don lit a cigarette and watched the screen closely. Slightly impatient for his favorite part of the film, he fast-forwarded and killed the sound. He had the screams memorized and had no need for auditory stimulation. The buxom redhead wearing a blindfold and purplish bruises across her face, breasts, buttocks and thighs was being dragged into the stark, cement block room. Her naked and hooded captors threw her on the darkly stained mattress that was lying on the cement floor abutting the far wall of the small room. A bare bulb swung from the ceiling, casting distorted shadows in the four corners of her holding cell. A rusty meat hook bolted high above the mattress next to a primitive crucifix were the room's only ornamentations.

The taller of the two men held a six-foot piece of rope and, kneeling beside his victim, he roughly grabbed her bruised wrists, tying them tightly together. The girl offered no resistance until she was yanked to her feet. She attempted to kick her captors but only succeeded in assaulting the air.

The two men easily lifted the girl and hung her by her wrists onto the meat hook, suspending her several inches from the floor and mattress.

Had Don left the volume on, he would have heard the girl scream, "No please stop!" over and over, followed by, "Please just kill me." Ignoring her plea, goon number one slapped her hard across her face.

Don chuckled, and said to the nameless girl, "Be careful what you wish for, cunt," and squashed his cigarette butt into the ashtray on his bedside table. He pushed down his boxers and began to stroke his fully aroused penis. He watched as the girl continued to get her face slapped and her nipple cruelly twisted and bit by one abuser, while her other tormentor roughly finger-fucked her.

Don worked his now throbbing, hard, red cock. Up and down, he pumped at a frenzied pace. He cupped and squeezed his balls keeping his eyes locked on the screen at the snuff porn that danced before him.

The tall, lead monster had grabbed a long knife from somewhere off-camera. Marching to his victim, he cut off her blindfold. Squinting and trying to adjust to the lighting, was a gorgeous doe-eyed female no older than twenty-one. No amount of bruising marred her beauty or her perfect, camera-ready makeup. Her captor showed her the gleaming, sharp, ten-inch blade as he placed the point of the knife against her breast, encircling her areola. Not cutting her skin, he ran the tip of the knife from her nipple down her body until he was inches from her beautifully shaved pussy. The other jackal pushed her thighs apart, to allow the knife entrance for blood to be spilled and purify her in her death.

"No!" she silently screamed pleading with her indifferent captor and beyond to the camera.

"Oh, yeah!" grunted Don as he pumped his cock one final time before he shook with orgasm, spewing his jizz all over his hand and computer. He wiped his hand on his bed sheet and quickly glanced at the screen. The girl hung lifeless from the hook, blood running from her pierced body, down her legs, across the mattress and dripped into the floor drain. *Got to love the special effects in snuff porn,* thought Don as he turned off the computer.

As the microwave signaled the end of the thawing process, Beth glanced at her phone. She was disappointed as well as surprised by Don's behavior, but she turned her focus to fixing dinner. She would deal with Don again after the kids were in bed. At least she knew he would be in Kendrick in three weeks' time for the party. They could begin to make some important decisions then. That reminded her, she needed to call Jess.

With dinner over and the boys tucked in, Beth had a shower and then snuggled into bed with the television on. Her first call was to Jess. She had a few ideas for the reception, but Jess made it clear that she would not be part of the planning process. The reception would be organized for her, and it would be revealed to the newlyweds once they arrived at the venue. The excitement that Jess shared was just the tonic Beth needed. After hanging up the phone, she felt cheerful and looking forward to having Don in Kendrick for the party. She hoped once she talked to Don, before turning in for the night, he would redeem himself and his attitude, and she could fall asleep in peace. Unfortunately, there would be no further communication between them that night. Although Beth had left several voicemail and text messages, all had gone unanswered.

She awoke with the same heavy heart as she had fallen asleep with. Turning over to face her bedside table, she immediately picked up her phone only to find no unanswered calls or messages. This was beginning to feel like the same bullshit that had prompted her to have a serious talk with Don in Vegas. *Had nothing changed?* Well, this time she would not continue to send him messages; she would wait and see how long it took him to respond. She was wide awake now and figured she may as well get up for the day. After a visit to the bathroom, she would have a cup of coffee, alone with her iPad until she had to get the boys up and moving for school. As a matter of fact, her phone would stay upstairs beside the bed. She was sick of checking it every five minutes. In fact, she was getting perturbed over a few things lately. So, Don was too busy to do some new house-hunting? Well, she was not! This had to become a priority. Not only would she soon put her own house up for sale, she would look into the Miami market herself. A realtor from Orlando she and Don had met in the Keys would help her out. At least, he could look at Don's house and give her an estimate of what it was worth, so she would have a ballpark price range. Don would probably thank her for releasing him from the house-hunting burden.

A good part of the day was over by the time Beth heard from her husband. Sensing her contempt for him, he quickly became aware that Beth was very unhappy at his lack of communication. Again, feigning that he had fallen asleep early, he begged forgiveness. She had no way of knowing otherwise, so instead of beleaguering the issue further, she gave in, changing the subject. His work was busy but going well. *Blah, blah, blah,* thought Beth to herself. She wished she found the financial and real estate development world interesting, but she just couldn't get into it. She preferred dealing with people, not blueprints or figures. Feeling better about finally connecting with Don, she was okay with hanging up and going on about her day.

Beth felt like she was in limbo. She had no intention of removing the boys from school until their year was complete, but that didn't mean they shouldn't start the process. She felt it was time to get the ball rolling, and it seemed up to her to throw the first pitch.

Chapter 5

The wedding reception at the club was only a few days away, and Don was due in Kendrick the next day. Beth could hardly wait. There was nothing better than having family and friends together. True to her word, Jess had not told Beth anything about the party. All the bride knew was what time to be there. The rest would be a surprise. One thing bothered her. How would Don and her sons interact now that they were legally a family? She was sure the kids' behavior toward him would be the same as it was during his last visit. She had reminded them that Don was coming to visit and the news hadn't fazed them a bit. Understandably, a legal piece of paper meant nothing to them. The onus was on Don. Would he pay them some attention? Would he try to get to know them? Would he want to enjoy some activities as a family? She hoped so, but realistically she knew she would probably have to guide the process – after all, Don had never done this sort of thing before.

Don's arrival day had come, and Beth was incredibly excited to be together with her husband. Close to a month had gone by since their wedding, and despite being occasionally disappointed by not being able to communicate with him, she had missed his touch and his loving. He had managed to book an early flight, so once the boys were on the bus, Beth said a hasty goodbye to Jess and went home to shower. The wedding reception was not until the following evening. Tonight would be family night. The four of them needed to spend time together if they were ever to feel like a family unit. Right now, Beth felt like the glue that held this shaky group together, but she wasn't strong enough to keep the status quo forever. She needed the kids to accept Don and allow him to provide the role of step-father; and she wanted to see Don step up and make an effort to be more than a husband. Only then could she relax and enjoy her new family without trying to artificially make it feel right.

Tonight, Don and the kids would enjoy dinner in the kitchen, then move to the family room for some home-spun family time where she and the kids had a surprise for him. She had briefed the kids on his arrival and had received little response. Encouraging her boys to talk with Don, she had suggested to them that they ask him about his home, his yacht, his swimming pool and the ocean. Beth knew that once she took the kids to Florida, even if only for a visit, it would all seem a little more real to them.

Don had not had a relaxing flight. Tension was building at work, and had he not thought it disastrous to cancel his own wedding reception, he would still be in Miami helping stabilize his business by dodging metaphorical land mines. Then, to add to his anxiety, he had nearly missed his connecting flight in Charlotte due to a late departure from Miami because of nearby lightning. Now that he was on the last leg of his journey, his thoughts turned to the stress ahead. He would soon have to deal with kids, probably unsupportive friends of Beth's, and learning the new roles of husband and step-father in order to play house. He knew the sex would be good, but other than that, there were few up sides to this mandatory visit. He longed for Miami already and quickly ordered a double Bourbon from the attractive flight attendant.

His wife was front and center as Don made his way among the other passengers through the terminal. Flinging her arms around him, she nearly knocked him off balance.

"Oh, baby, am I glad to see you," whispered Beth, as she nibbled on his ear.

"Me too," said Don, running both hands all over Beth's ass while he held her tightly against him. For a few moments, he forgot about Miami as his lower brain took over and began to signal his cock to get ready. Beth was feeling something solid against her abdomen causing her nipples to stiffen under her emerald green, skin-tight tank top. The protruding nipples assured Don she had dressed braless, and as he felt her ass, he had a sneaky suspicion she was also commando. He had no trouble visualizing her without the top and clingy, black bike shorts, and with her long, curly, red hair extensions, he was already revved up and raring to go!

She had made him sit back in the car's passenger seat while she drove them home. He had figured conversation would center on discussing the next evening's party and the kids, but to his delight, she only wanted to talk dirty to him all the way home. He so badly wanted to feel her crotch and tweak those nipples that were straining to be freed, but she would not allow any of it. Instead, she, forced both their libidos to wait until the front door closed behind them. Even then, she had postponed sex by grabbing his hand and leading him up to the master suite. She had taken a cue from Tom and had placed masculine soap, lotion, deodorant and silk boxers in her bathroom and closet. Now, he would know that it was no longer her domain but theirs.

Don had quickly assessed and properly thanked her for the grooming products and clothing while he flung her onto the bed pulling down her tank top, unceremoniously revealing her round, fair-skinned breasts with their delicate, pink nipples. *Oh, yeah,* thought Don, *this is so much better than the whores on Biscayne Boulevard or the professionals at the Miami strip clubs.* He hadn't fucked her since consummating their marriage back in Vegas, and now he was going to make up for it. Their video cam sex had satiated him only temporarily. Every day, he had masturbated numerous times while he thought about sweet, little Beth playing with herself for pleasure. Yeah, he had watched lots of online porn in the past month, and although his favorite escorts treated him well, as always, he had been excited to get together with Beth. They had a familiar sex history by now. It had been somewhat tedious teaching her what he liked, but now it was paying off; and as they continued to explore their sexual boundaries, he would teach her more.

His tongue attacked her breasts and his fingers found her crotch, but just as he was about to pull down her tight, ass-hugging shorts, she quickly moved so that now he was on the bottom. Through his khaki shorts, she massaged his cock, taking it from hard to rigid. While she fumbled with his button and fly, she pressed her mouth against his, positioning her breasts within cupping distance. Just as she schemed, he grabbed both and manipulated them with a slightly rough attitude. It wasn't so much that the sex was hurried but rather that it was intense.

Both participants were serious, engaged, yet almost mechanical. They were there for a purpose. To relieve built-up sexual tension, making conversation unnecessary and romance optional. Gestures were all that were needed, each letting the other know with body language what was expected. Even Beth, usually the romantic, was more interested in reaching orgasm with a cock tight in her pussy than pillow talk or gentle caresses. Now he was suspended on top of her, and that's where he would stay. He reacted by plunging his rod directly into her wet hole. The assault felt just as good to her as it did to him. His eyes fixated on hers were equally as unwavering. This intense coupling was within seconds of being over. Beth felt the warmth spread throughout her pelvis, and an intense throbbing twinned with a reflexive cry indicating she had reached orgasm. Her timing was impeccable. She had faintly heard Don gasp as he completed his mission. He leaned heavily on his hands that were now positioned beside each of her shoulders on the bright white sheet. There! The necessary physical release was over, and the couple could turn their attention to everything else.

"That was just what I needed from my husband."

"Yes, Mrs. Lyons, that felt real good," replied Don as he rolled off his wife onto the bed beside her. She found his hand and laced her fingers in his as they both focused on the ceiling.

"I need to use the bathroom. Then I think a quick shower is in order for me," said Beth, as she made no attempt to get up.

"You go ahead. I just want to lie here awhile. I'll take my turn once you're done in there."

Hating the thought of getting off the bed, Beth lay there for several more minutes, resting with her eyes closed. "Tonight we're staying home. How handy are you with a grill?"

"I can hold my own. What's do you have planned?"

"I'm going to marinate some chicken, if you would

start the grill and cook it."

"I can handle that," assured Don.

"Once I'm out of the shower, I'll start making salads. When the boys get off the bus, they are usually starving, so I like to feed them by five."

"Sure, whatever," replied Don. Beth let go of his hand, leaned over and gave her husband a quick peck. Then she got out of bed and headed to the bathroom. Once Don heard the shower door shut, he picked up his phone with business being the only thing on his mind.

With dinner over, Beth tried to get the boys to hang out with her and Don. In her mind, tonight was going to be family time, but staging the evening made it awkward. Matt and Max would seldom sit in the family room unless there was something interesting to watch on television. After several minutes of stilted conversation and deafening silence, Beth realized she had to let this new family unit establish itself over time. But that didn't mean she would give up trying to nurture a relationship between her husband and her sons. The kids took off upstairs immediately when Beth dismissed them from what they must have felt was detention. Giving the kids some time to get involved in an activity in their room, Beth convinced Don to follow them and join in with whatever they were doing.

Don could hardly tell Beth he had no desire to play with her kids or anybody else's. He was officially the boys' step-dad, and this new role was one he dreaded. While Beth remained on the couch, Don reluctantly started up the stairs to the sound of chatter. He found them sitting on the floor building with their Lego blocks.

"Hi, guys, what are you building?" At the sight and

sound of the veritable stranger, both boys ceased conversation and all activity. Their look screamed, *what are you doing here, and what do you want?*

"Would you mind if I joined you? Maybe I can help build," offered Don. The two boys exchanged looks of confusion mixed with suspicion. Matt's eyes darted back to the blocks on the carpet, making it clear he would let his older brother do the talking with the intruder.

"I guess so," said Max, as he shrugged his shoulders in defeat. Knowing the answer was hardly an invitation but the best he would get, Don ventured in and then sat down on the floor, opposite the kids.

"So, what are you building here?" he repeated.

"We're building a barn for these," said Max motioning to the small, plastic, farmyard animals that lay in a heap nearby.

"I'd like to help, if you tell me what to do."

"Well, we need another wall built like this one."

"Could we put some windows in it, so the cows and horses would have some light in their barn?"

"Oh yeah, that would be cool." And with that, Don had ingratiated his way into a tiny piece of the boys' lives.

Beth, afraid to disturb whatever was going on up there, was pleased that ten minutes had gone by, and Don had not yet made his escape. Eventually, curiosity got the better of her, and she grabbed her phone from the coffee table making her way up the stairs. As she peered into Max's room, the scene before her warmed her heart. All three of her men were engrossed as a team. She couldn't help but snap a few pictures of the domestic bliss. So far, this was the highlight of Don's visit. Before long, she would have to break up the Lego engineers as bedtime for everyone was fast approaching.

Chapter 6

It was Friday morning, and the wedding reception was later that evening. Beth woke up in a fabulous mood fueled by how well Max, Matt, and Don had interacted the night before. She almost regretted the inability of the kids to attend the evening's festivities. She could begin to visualize them as a family now, and it was unfortunate that the evening's celebration was adult only. Before they could leave for Climax, she and the boys would have a surprise for Don. At least the boys could be a part of this.

Beth wanted to walk to the Johnsons' and touch base with Jess to discuss whatever she might learn about the evening's upcoming activities. Following breakfast, Don actually agreed to accompany Beth and the boys to Jess's. As they knocked quietly, and then let themselves into the house, Jess was curious when she heard voices. Coming out of the kitchen to see who it was, she was somewhat surprised to see Don up and about with Beth and the boys. During a quick cup of coffee with Jess, Beth was disappointed that her friend was still keeping mum about any party details. After seeing the boys off on the school bus, they took another few minutes to empty their cups and then made their way back to Beth's. This morning's coffee break was brief since Beth had a hair appointment and manicure scheduled in preparation for the reception. She also needed to pick up both their outfits from the tailor. She had insisted on buying Don's new suit for him. A small token – a wedding gift. She was excited to get her dress back from being altered. It had fit perfectly except for the sleeve and hem length. The dress made her feel very sexy, and she knew Don would approve. She hadn't seen the suit that Don had chosen but knew it was Armani, made of virgin wool. They would see each other in their reception attire for the first time when they were ready to leave the house.

Jason, her sons' favorite babysitter, was coming over, so the kids would eat pizza. Between the boys returning home from school and Jason appearing, Don's surprise would take place. Beth was just as excited for this as for the reception.

With her errands completed, Beth returned home with her hair in a sleek up do, her nails perfect, carrying two garment bags, which she immediately hung in the bedroom closet. Returning to the main floor, she found Don dozing on the family room sofa. She stood beside him, smiling down at her man. A snapshot from a Norman Rockwell calendar – just the way she hoped their life would be. She hated to wake him but just couldn't resist bending down to brush his lips with her own – soft as a feather. He stirred briefly, adjusted his position slightly, but continued to sleep. She tiptoed away knowing once the boys returned home from school, there would be no rest for anyone.

Beth quietly closed the front door behind her as she left to pick up the kids. Thankfully, there was no wind, so messing her new hair style was not a worry. She had purposefully left a little early, so she could check in with Jess. She was buzzing with excitement and knew her friend would be as well. Beth opened the front door to learn that Eric was home with the three boys while Jess had gone to the club to help get things ready for the night's celebration. Saying goodbye to Ben and Eric, Beth and her boys made their way home. Beth knew her kids would miss Ben the most. He was a year older than Max but had been the boys' buddy since they were born.

As predicted, once the front door opened and two exuberant boys entered, Don had no choice but to wake up. As he yawned and stretched, Beth ordered him to remain on the couch while she herded her sons up to her bedroom. Once inside, she told them to sit quietly on the bed and listen. The kids exchanged puzzled looks, rolling their eyes at their mother's unexplained seriousness.

"Okay, guys. The three of us are going to give Don a very special gift. When people get married, they give each other wedding rings. See," said Beth, holding out her left hand. "When Don and I got married, he gave me this, but I didn't have time to get him one. But once he went back to Miami, I had time to shop, and I bought him a wedding ring, too. You boys and I are his family now, so I thought it would be nice if the ring came from all three of us."

"Does that mean we are married to Don, too?" asked Max, trying to put two and two together.

"Well, not exactly. I married him, so that makes him your step-dad, and you two are his step-children. If we all give him this ring, it will mean we are a family."

"Oh, okay," replied Max. Matt seemed somewhat oblivious as to what was going on, but if his big brother played along, so would he.

Beth reached into her top dresser drawer and removed a black, square jewelry box, motioning to the boys to follow her downstairs. Don was sitting on the sofa with the remote in his hand flipping through the channels. He briefly looked up when he saw the entourage approaching.

Beth sat down next to him, removed the device from his hand, effectively shutting off the television, and motioned for the boys to perch on the coffee table in front of her and Don.

"Now, what's going on here?" asked Don.

"We have a present for you," answered Matt.

"Oh, really? That's cool."

"Don," said Beth, seriously, "you were so thoughtful and generous when you purchased this exquisite wedding band for me, and I love it. I felt badly that I hadn't done the same for you. The boys and I have something very important to give you."

"It's a ring," said Matt spilling the beans while his older brother lightly poked him in the ribs with his elbow.

"Shut up, Matt," scolded Max.

"It's okay, boys," assured Beth. She handed the box to Don, who opened it slowly.

"Let me put it on you," said Beth as she removed it and slipped it on his left hand. As Don bent toward Beth, she stopped him. "I want to explain the significance of this ring. First of all, the setting is platinum. That stands for you. Very strong yet beautiful and precious. As you can see, it holds the center part of the ring. The middle of the band is made up of three types of metal braided together. There is yellow, white, and rose gold. Those signify the boys and me. The fact that they are braided says we are stronger when together. The fit is a comfort band. I hope it means we will all become very comfortable with our new family roles as time goes by. Please accept this from the boys and me as a symbol of how happy we are to be a new family together." Beth concluded the description with a catch in her voice, trying not to cry as she finished her emotional speech.

Looking down at his hand, Don had to admit it was a

very handsome ring and looked good on his tanned finger. He couldn't help but wonder how much it was worth. Don reached forward and gathered Beth and the two, somewhat reluctant, boys into a hug, thanking them for the thoughtful gift.

"Jason will be here before long, and I need to get ready," said Beth as she started toward the stairs. Don knew that even if he took a shower, he would still be ready before Beth, so he settled back on the sofa instructing one of the kids to grab a beer for him from the kitchen fridge.

Beth only needed to worry about her clothes and makeup. Because of her trip to the hair salon, she was able to sidestep dealing with her long hair. The weather was beautiful, and even with the cooler evening air, she knew she could comfortably go bare-legged. As she undressed, she pondered what set of lingerie to wear under her gorgeous cocktail dress. She decided on the nude panty that she had worn when Tom had visited her home. She had paid a fortune for it and had purchased it just for their rendezvous. *Why did so many things bring up memories of Tom? Of all times for him to come to mind,* she reprimanded herself. She slipped on the underwear, luxuriating in it for just a minute. No matter how she turned to look at herself, she could not find a bad view of her own reflection. Beth made her way into the master closet to find the garment bags that hung side by side. Unzipping the white one, she couldn't help but run her fingers over the hand-beading on the dress; then she removed it from the bag.

As she carefully slid the shoulders off the hanger, the weight of the dress surprised her. The entire champagne-colored dress was adorned with gold and ivory beads in intricate patterns. Beth stepped into the dress, adjusted it over her hips and then closed the ornate button at the back of the Mandarin collar. The dress was a sheath, ending a couple of inches above her knee. It had long sleeves, and the front ended at a high neckline. The back of the dress was a show-stopper. The entire back was cut out from the waist up to the collar. The fit was exquisite. Mind you, what she had paid for the alterations was almost as much as the cost of the dress itself. She had chosen to wear gold stilettos and carry a delicate, gold evening bag.

Next came her makeup. Spending more time than usual, she used bolder colors and a heavier hand, knowing it was an evening event and so much attention would be directed at her. Last, but not least, she put on her gold and diamond chandelier earrings. They had been a very generous gift from her parents when she had graduated with her master's degree and had not been outside her safe for many years. At the last minute, she wedged her way into her high heels. Then tossing lip gloss into her evening bag, she sauntered down the stairs hoping her sultry entrance would not be wasted. As Don heard her approaching, he turned toward her and let loose a long, slow, wolf whistle.

"Wow! I'm sure glad you're my date tonight!"

"And your wife," reminded Beth as Don stood up and walked toward her. He picked up her free hand and twirled her around, so he could get a 360 degree view.

"Your wedding dress was exquisite, but this dress is stunning. I love the back!"

"Why, thank you. Now I think you better get a move on, too," said Beth, as she playfully smacked him on the butt with her evening bag. "Your suit and shirt are in the closet in the black garment bag," she instructed.

Don had not seen his suit yet. He had chosen the

color, the fit, the fabric and the tailor. Then he had faxed his measurements to a well-known men's store in Kendrick. He had known the color of Beth's dress and had the salesman help him in selecting not only the suit but also the shirt and tie.

After turning on the shower, Don found the garment bag and laid its contents across the bed. *Very, very nice,* he thought to himself with approval. Knowing he was going to look very handsome, he confidently stepped under the water. Within a few minutes, he, had scrubbed, shaved and dried off. The suit was a camel color, and he could tell by the feel of the slacks next to his skin that it was a very rich material. The shirt was a deep cream color with just the slightest hint of peach. The tie was of a neutral palette with metallic gold thread running through it. Looking at himself in the mirror, he knew he looked good and would have Beth's approval.

The animated chatter he could hear from the top of the stairs meant that Jason had arrived; therefore, their evening could begin. He found all four of them in the kitchen where Beth was giving directions about plates and cutlery but wisely standing far back from the sloppy pizza sitting on the counter. She looked up when she heard his footsteps and gasped.

"Oh, babe, you look amazing," she said while quickly walking to him, cutlery clutched in her hand. She stopped in front of him and inhaled deeply. Beth loved the fragrance of his cologne and took another smell before kissing him on the lips.

"Wow, Mr. Lyons, looking good," said Jason, admiring the slim fitting suit.

"Why, thank you, Jason."

"I think we make a very handsome couple," said Beth, as she posed beside him as if there were a camera pointing at them.

"With or without our clothes," whispered Don into her ear, making her cheeks flush.

"It looks like everything here is under control, so I guess we can get going," said Beth, surveying the kitchen table where the kids were already devouring their pizza. Grabbing their coats, keys, and Beth's evening bag, the Lyons made their way to Club Climax.

Chapter 7

on and Beth had been told little about their reception other than to make an entrance at a specified time. Typically, they would have been at the club earlier, but tonight the dinner and dance was a private affair, so the usual club schedule did not apply. Pulling into the parking lot, they noticed there were more vehicles than on other nights. Was it because it was a little later than usual, or were there more people because of the party? That was yet to be determined.

Instead of walking through the club's front door past Kristie's podium, they walked around to a side door that opened directly into the banquet room. The room for rent had been constructed so those invited to events, but not club members or guests, could attend and feel at home.

Don opened the door, and Beth walked into a medium-sized room that glowed. She stopped dead in her tracks, barely in the room far enough to allow Don a view. Someone had done an amazing job decorating. Although Beth had never seen the banquet room prior to tonight, she could only presume it had been a stark room with a hardwood floor, white walls, and nondescript folding tables and chairs. Her eyes didn't know where to look first. The round tables were beautifully set, a small table off to the side looked to have a cake perched on it, and even the ceiling had been transformed. Beth reached behind her and grabbed Don's hand at just about the time Jess and Cindy noted their arrival. The two friends came scurrying over to the honored couple, hugging Beth while offering the groom their congratulations.

"This is the most beautiful place I've ever seen," Beth said, as she swiped away a lone tear.

"Crying's not allowed," said Jess definitively. "Come on, you two. We're dying to show you around." They started at the back of the room where Kristie had volunteered to sit at the guest book, instructing those invited to sign and telling them where to place their wedding gifts. Each round table for six featured a crisp, white, linen cloth. In the center of the table sat a tall centerpiece that held creamy-white tapers surrounded by lush cream and pale peach roses, white hydrangeas with ivy entangling them all. A gold charger topped with a white plate and polished, silver cutlery sat ready for each diner. Every chair was encased with a white, floor-length cover with tiny pleats all around the skirt.

The bride and groom's table also sat six, and Beth was happy to see, by the place cards, that Jess and Eric and Jack and Cindy would dine with them. Their table boasted a shimmering gold table cloth, with the same dishes and cutlery. The other difference was the monogrammed champagne flutes sitting next to the plates of the bride and groom.

Cindy instructed Beth and Don to look up. In the center of the ceiling was a massive chandelier. Where its mounting hugged the ceiling, yards and yards of white organza had been draped and secured in each corner of the room. The walls had also been draped in pleated organza with tiny, white lights nestled in the folds, adding subtle sparkle everywhere. Cindy and Jess had saved the best for last. The wedding cake sat off to the side, by itself, knowing full well the spotlight would be on it eventually. It was not tall or ornate. Quite the opposite. It had two round layers, covered in a cream-colored fondant, making it appear as though it were covered in satin rather than a sugary paste. Both tiers were covered with intricate piping resembling lace, and instead of the traditional bride and groom figurines, the cake top featured a small bouquet of cream-colored, peach-edged roses. A perfect, elegant top for a beautiful, elegant cake. An engraved gold knife and cake server sat beside the confection waiting to assist in the sharing, allowing each guest to enjoy a taste.

By now, everyone knew the bride and groom had arrived. Beth and Don found themselves surrounded by well-wishers. The open bar was pouring champagne among other libations, and someone had thoughtfully placed a glass of the bubbly into the hands of the newly married couple. After several more minutes of mingling, they heard the sound of a microphone being turned on as Jack welcomed the crowd and encouraged the guests to find their seats for dinner. Following a sumptuous meal of prime rib, chicken cordon bleu, and an assortment of side dishes, Jack announced the cutting of the cake. Camera flashes twinkled among the crowd capturing the moment when Beth playfully smeared frosting on Don's face. Knowing better to than to ruin's Beth's makeup, Don, wisely, did not reciprocate.

The music began, and the bride and groom took to the dance floor. They definitely made a handsome couple – even Tom had to admit it, if only to himself. Once the song ended, Beth and Don took control of the microphone thanking everyone for their efforts. With that, the more formal part of the evening ended, and a relaxed party atmosphere took over.

Don's bride was a knockout in her short, form-fitting

dress, but Don could not keep his eyes off Kristie. He had noticed that after the first dance ended, she had vanished. He casually inquired about her whereabouts and was told she had resumed her duties at the club's front door podium. He had thoroughly enjoyed being between Kristie and Beth before, and knew he wouldn't have many more opportunities once Beth moved to Florida, so tonight seemed like a logical time to ask Kristie for a repeat performance.

Beth was surrounded by female guests anxious to hear all the details of their wedding and plans for the future. She wouldn't notice him slipping out into the club. Don made his way toward the front of the building. Sure enough, there was the ever dutiful Kristie in her greeter role.

"Hey, Kristie, too bad you had to leave the party."

"Oh, hi, Don," said Kristie, a little surprised to see him. "Your guests had all arrived, so I thought I would be more useful here."

"I can think of plenty of uses for you," winked Don. A troubling look overtook her face as Don continued. "You wouldn't be interested in a playroom would you?"

"What!" said Kristie, knowing she had heard correctly, yet not quite believing it.

"Well, this is a sex club, after all. We've had some fun together in the past."

"I think it's inappropriate for you to think about playing with anyone except your beautiful wife tonight. It's practically your wedding night. Is Beth okay with this?"

"Beth is busy with a bunch of women right now. But if you want a threesome, I'll approach her about it."

"Don, I don't want sex at all from you – certainly not tonight!"

"That's fine. I just thought I would ask. Let's keep this between you and me. Beth needn't know I spoke to you." Without answering him, Kristie turned her back to Don as she heard the club's door open and guests enter.

Naturally, Tom and Rosa had been invited to the party. It was common knowledge among club members that Beth and Tom shared a sexual history, swinger style. Few, however, knew their sexual relationship had also included numerous, private rendezvous at a pricey penthouse that Tom had rented exclusively for those occasions. Tom had always felt protective of Beth, and his concern for her had escalated exponentially when she began a relationship with Don Lyons. So, when Tom accidentally witnessed Don hitting on Kristie at her podium, he stepped back into the shadows, just far enough away that he wouldn't be detected yet close enough to be able to hear their conversation.

Tom was not as surprised as Kristie was at Don's unwarranted invitation. Tom sensed that Don only showed some of his persona to Beth and her friends, and that there was more to this man than anyone in Kendrick knew. Tom was on a mission to rectify that. He had Don pegged as a greedy low-life, and the combination of the man's gluttony and low intelligence would be his undoing. Someone just had to set the bait.

While Kristie attended to the new arrivals, and Don made a U-turn back to the party, Tom, undetected, stepped out from the shadows. He had an offer he knew Don couldn't and wouldn't resist.

"Hey, Don," called out Tom, as he hastened his pace to catch up to the groom. "I haven't properly congratulated you on your marriage. You couldn't have chosen a lovelier lady, my friend," said Tom while he held out his hand for a congratulatory shake. "You probably know that I think

Beth is very special, so I'd like to offer the two of you a vacation as a wedding gift. My wife and I own several houses abroad, and one happens to be in the Bahamas. We'd be delighted if the two of you would agree to use it, free of charge, of course."

"Wow," said Don, "that's really generous of you."

"Oh, not really. It sits vacant much of the time. Just give me your email address, and I'll send you its availability. Once you two have picked out some dates, email them to me, and I'll set it up." Tom wrote down Don's email address, folding the scrap of paper and slipping it into his suit jacket pocket. As he did, he mentally checked a box.

Don slinked back into the banquet room where he stopped at the bar. As his martini was being shaken, not stirred, he scanned the crowd for Beth. She remained chatting amicably, seemingly unaware of his recent departure. Just as he picked up his glass, his phone vibrated in his pocket. Retrieving it quickly, he sputtered, "Oh, shit," to no one in particular as he recognized the caller's number. Knowing he had to take the call, he gulped down his martini in one swig, put his phone to his ear, and quickly made his way to the men's room for some quiet and privacy.

"*Hola*," said Don, "*si, si, sé que estoy atrasado en el pago.*" After listening for a moment, he answered, "*No, no lo hagas nada drastico. Te juro que voy a tener el dinero pronto.*" As he listened to the reply, he began to sweat and his tone changed to a pleading desperation. "*Debo tener una o dos semanas mas,*" promised Don as he nervously fingered his new wedding band. "*Si, si, gracias. No voy a defraudar a su. Adios.*" Don took the phone from his ear, looked at it for several seconds, placed it back in his jacket pocket, and walked to one of the granite sinks.

Turning on the cold water, he splashed some on his face, not caring that some trickled onto his beautiful wool suit. He dried his face and hands with a couple of paper towels, then placed his hands on either side of the wet sink, leaning heavily on the vanity. His gaze rose to the small, square mirror hanging slightly askew in front of him. He felt pale and looked it. Taking a deep, cleansing breath, he adjusted his tie and walked back into the party. He had just been given a reprieve but wasn't feeling relieved. In fact, terror was more like it. As he stepped back into the party, he pasted a smile on his face; he knew he could fake anything.

As the bathroom door automatically shut behind Don, a toilet flushed behind a stall's closed door. Someone had heard and understood Don's side of the conversation. Now, that someone had to decide what to do with the new, interesting information. Washing his hands at the same sink as Don had pondered his phone call, Eric was deep in thought. It seemed either Don didn't realize the stall had been occupied or he assumed the Spanish language would be foreign to the man using the toilet. Had Don seen Eric in the bathroom, he would not have thought the man would know Spanish. With his reddish hair and blue eyes, he looked Irish through and through. But Eric had grown up a military brat. His father had enjoyed a career in the Coast Guard, and the family had been stationed in Puerto Rico for many years. Eric was as fluent in Spanish as he was in English.

He realized that he had only been privy to one side of the conversation, but Don's tone of voice did not shroud how troubling the call had been for him. Eric knew that Beth presumed Don to be wealthy, far from having financial difficulties, but the phone call indicated otherwise. Of course, he couldn't know from the few sentences he had heard how much money he owed or to whom he owed it. It sounded like the person had given Don a couple of weeks to pay it back, and Don had sounded relieved.

Eric's gut told him he had to share this information. He thought of going to Beth, but what if it boiled down to just business? What if he was making more of it than it was worth? No, he'd somehow get Don investigated first before he troubled the new bride with any information. Then he thought of Randy. It was easy to forget that he was a police detective. He was so good at changing his persona to reflect a good ole' Southern boy just pouring libations. As Eric left the men's room, he paused scanning the room for Randy. Tonight, he was not volunteering at the bar but was Beth's invited guest. There he was, with his girlfriend, Laura, leaning on the bar. Eric casually walked up to the couple.

"Hey, Randy, Laura," said Eric.

"Hey, dude," replied Randy as he shook Eric's hand. "Nice party."

"Yes, it's great. Cindy and Jess did a good job putting it all together. Hey, Randy, can I talk to you in private for just a minute?"

"Sure, excuse us, baby," Randy said to Laura, as he patted her behind. "What's up?"

"I just overheard something in the men's room that is troubling. You are more of an expert about these things than I am, so I wanted to run it by you." As Randy listened to the description of the brief conversation Eric had overheard, the hair on his arms stood on end. He and Tom had discussed Don, and he knew Tom didn't believe much the guy said. Now, Randy thought Tom and Eric might be on to something.

"If I could get his driver's license number, I could run

him in the system and see if anything comes up."

"I don't know how we could get his license."

"Leave that to me. I'll let you know what I find out."

"Thanks, Randy. None of us wants to see Beth hurt," said Eric as he extended his hand in appreciation. Randy stood motionless for a moment, not so much to ponder what he had just heard but to calculate his next move. No doubt Don would only be in town a short time, so he had to move fast. *No time like the present,* said Randy to himself, as he scanned the room for the bridegroom.

Don had been cornered by some of the club's matriarchs including its owner, Jezzy. He didn't know any of them, and their nosey questions and tireless chatter had been trying his patience for far too long. It was with relief and a feeling of being rescued when he saw Randy approaching. Cutting off an admirer mid-sentence, Don took a step forward.

"Now, here's a fellow I haven't had a chance to speak to all evening." Randy shook Don's hand, and although Don expected the gaggle of women to move away, they instead quickly gathered Randy into their fold.

"Congratulations, Don, you're a lucky man."

"Don't I know it?"

"I hear it all took place in Vegas. You wouldn't happen to have any pictures would you?"

"You'll have to ask Beth. She has...no, wait a minute. I do have a couple in my wallet." This was just what Randy was hoping for. He was also hoping the license would be front and center in Don's billfold. And it was. At this point, the women crowded closer to Don, all wanting a good look at the two wedding pictures. This forced Don to keep his wallet open for the better part of a minute making it easy for Randy to memorize the unique identification. Mission accomplished!

The remainder of the evening went well. Beth and Don enjoyed being the center of attention and the food, drink, music as well as the company had been top notch. As the night wound down, and guests began to leave, Beth and Don sat with Jess and Cindy and their husbands. The Lyons couldn't thank them enough for the beautiful evening they had planned and executed and all three couples agreed they would meet at the club the following night. With Don's time in Kendrick short, opportunities to be together were rare. The bartender had just announced last call, signaling a good end to the evening. The party had been fun, but two little boys would be up in another five or so hours.

Chapter 8

No sex at the club with Kristie had made Don a horny boy, and he took delight on relieving his disappointment once they got home from the party. Forgetting that the kids could interrupt their sleep, Don coerced his tired wife into having sex. Wound up from adrenaline and champagne, Beth would not have hesitated while they were at the club, but the ride home had given the alcohol time to act like the depressive it was. The booze, the motion of the car, the darkness and the late hour had lulled Beth into a half sleep. Removing her party outfit and settling into bed was what she was looking forward to.

"How about a quickie when we get home?" Don suggested. Beth paused, reached over to pat his leg, and responded, "I don't know if I have the energy, sweetie. I am dog tired."

"Does that mean we can do it doggie-style?" asked Don.

"Very funny."

"C'mon, watching you all night in that sexy dress, how did you think I'd react?"

"Remember, we have kids who are going to be up in a few hours," reminded Beth.

"It won't take me long. You know that," countered Don. It was clear to Beth that he was only thinking of his own quick orgasm. This had nothing to do with her. She felt like she could have been a blow-up doll, and he would have ended up equally satisfied. The gnawing feeling of disappointment troubled her stomach once again, tarnishing what had been an evening to remember.

They said good night to Jason, reminding him that they would see him again the following night. With the house locked up, the Lyons retreated to the master suite. Once ready for bed, Beth climbed in naked, giving herself over to the inevitable. Don was true to his word. He had kissed her, fondled her breasts until he was hard, plunged his cock into her and, after thrusting a few times, he exploded, filling her with his juice. All the while, she lay on her back looking at the ceiling, tears filling her eyes. As he rolled off, he gave her a quick kiss and muttered, "Good night." His blow-up doll lay beside him totally deflated.

The kids mercifully slept in a couple of hours later than usual, giving Beth more sleep than she had anticipated. Don was still sound asleep when she crept out of bed, grabbed a robe, and said good morning to Max and Matt. They followed her downstairs to the kitchen where she immediately got the coffee pot going. The kids had asked for pancakes, and she set about, grudgingly, to prepare them. She knew she was upset with Don, but it was difficult not to take her disappointment and frustration out on those around her.

Not only had Don slept an additional two hours more than her that morning, but he had also gone for an afternoon nap before Jason had arrived. Beth had not had that luxury and had felt fatigued throughout the day. The shower she had taken prior to dressing for the club had perked her up somewhat while Don looked and felt well-rested. Don was excited in more ways than one to head to Club Climax. He would approach Beth and Kristie about a threesome. He had had that image in his head all day and was counting on making it a reality.

Randy was back at his usual seat behind the club's bar. Eric and Jess had just shed their coats and were heading to order a cocktail. Eric and Randy locked eyes for a second, long enough for Eric to know Randy had information. Randy remained focused on pouring drinks for the large crowd, unable to get a moment to talk to Eric in private. But as dinnertime approached, the crowd thinned as guests began taking their seats. Eric and Jess joined Beth and Don at a table, and when Jess excused herself to use the ladies' room, Eric took the opportunity to head back to the bar.

"Hey, man," he said to Randy, "I've got a minute. What did you find out?"

"Nothin' yet, absolutely nothing by way of his license. I'm going to get some fingerprints from him tonight and run those. I'm not giving up yet," assured Randy.

"That's my man," said Eric with a smile. "Talk to you later."

After dinner, Don and Beth, with drinks in hand, walked outside to the patio. They were stopped by members congratulating them on their marriage and thanking them for the great party the night before. Don still had Kristie on his mind and excused himself from the conversation to head to the podium, stopping on the way for a fresh drink.

"What can I get you?"

"I'd like another one of these, if you don't mind."

"No problem," said Randy as he fixed the drink,

pushing the glass toward Don. Just as Don picked up the glass, Randy's brow furrowed. "Sorry, bud, your glass is dirty," immediately snatching it from Don, pouring out the contents and fixing him another drink. "I apologize. Can't seem to get good help around here," he joked.

"Not a problem," replied Don as he took his new drink and headed toward the front door. Randy carefully picked up Don's dirty glass with a pair of tongs, putting it in a paper bag, and placing it under the bar. Tomorrow, the glass would be processed at the police station where Don's fingerprints would be lifted.

Before Don could offer another invitation to Kristie, Beth had caught up to him.

"Hey, handsome, can I talk to you for a minute? There is something I've been thinking about."

"Of course, babe."

"I know we are both swingers, but I'm wondering how you would feel about changing some boundaries now that we are married."

"What did you have in mind?"

"I've read that a lot of married couples have a no penetration rule. Everything is fair game up until actual intercourse. They save that for each other, exclusively. What do you think?"

"I don't have a problem with that. I would much rather fuck my wife than anyone else anyway."

"Oh, Don, I love you so much. I was worried you would think it was ridiculous."

Don had no problem agreeing to the rule. After all, what he did in Florida, or behind closed doors without her, she didn't need to worry her pretty little red head about.

"No, it's not ridiculous. Our marriage is a new beginning, so there is nothing wrong with new rules." *Except now I won't be fucking fuckalicious Kristie tonight,* thought Don. "Doesn't mean you and I can't enjoy the club tonight," said Don, as he fondled his wife's breast.

"You read my mind, hubby."

"Any thoughts about a threesome?" asked Don, still hoping to at least get his hands on Kristie.

"Yes. My thoughts are no. I want you to myself. I've got big plans for you, tiger."

"Grrr," growled Don, as they walked to a playroom.

Beth led Don to the room with the sex chair and king sized bed. She had fond memories of when Jess and Eric had titillated her in the very same chair. She had hoped she could give Don an experience to remember, too.

"So, what's the big surprise?" questioned Don.

"I need you to sit down in the chair," said Beth. "But you have to take off your clothes first," she grinned. "I'll shut the blinds and close the door."

Wanting this stupid game over with, Don stripped down and sat in the chair.

"Now what?" he asked as pleasantly as possible.

"I'm going to blindfold you and just loosely tie you to the chair."

Don sat wordlessly, which Beth took as consent. She slid the black fabric blindfold over Don's eyes. Beth then slipped both wrists and ankles into the leather restraints but did not tighten them. She had already placed a riding crop, feather tickler, and a bucket of ice in the room.

She removed her clothing until she was wearing just bra and panties, then knelt between Don's legs, causing Don to jump slightly.

"Shh, it's just me. Relax," said Beth in a soft whisper.

She grabbed a few ice cubes and swirled them around her mouth until she was sure her tongue was cooled. She grasped Don's flaccid penis and pumped it with a tightened grip. Not getting the reaction she had hoped for, she decided to try a more indirect approach.

She crouched forward and lightly licked Don's nipple with her cold tongue. Then she heard Don suck in his breath. *Now I'm getting somewhere,* hoped Beth. She continued flicking her tongue back and forth between his nipples and reached for the feather tickler. She lightly touched his shoulder, and immediately saw Don stiffen and sit straighter. Beth began tracing light, circular patterns across his chest, arms, thighs, and calves with the feather, purposely avoiding his still flaccid penis.

Looking down at his crotch, she thought, *why not?* And began stroking the length of his cock with the tip of the feather. Still no response.

Beth threw down the tickler down and grabbed the riding crop. She lightly slapped Don across the forearm and immediately kissed the red welt.

"That is goddamn enough!" shouted Don as he pulled his ankles and wrists from the shackles and threw off his blindfold. Beth was thrown to the floor as Don abruptly stood up.

"What's wrong?" asked Beth with tears forming in her eyes.

"You want to get fucked, then let's fuck," said Don as he reached down and yanked Beth rather unceremoniously onto her feet, then flinging her to her back onto the bed. Pinning her hands above her head against the mattress, he seethed, "You like being restrained and roughed up, is that it? Well, I don't!"

"No," stammered Beth. I was trying to turn you on – the whole pleasure-pain principle. The unknown of what was coming next."

"Fuck that shit, Beth," said Don.

Don kissed her roughly, but Beth did not kiss him back. He rolled her over onto her stomach and spreading her legs, pulled her panties to the side and rammed his engorged, throbbing pole inside her. Beth was not ready and certainly not lubricated. Her eyes opened wide with surprise and shock as he pressed her now loosened hand over her mouth, so she couldn't yell out in pain. After a few thrusts, Don grunted, and she felt his cum ooze out across her thigh as his withering cock slid back out.

He flopped onto the bed beside her and looking up at the ceiling said, "Sorry. Please don't ever piss me off like that again."

Instead of feeling fulfilled and closer to her husband because of a great sexual encounter, Beth felt violated and bullied. While Don occupied the adjoining bathroom, she lay on the club's bed trying to make sense of what had just happened. She wracked her brain going over the encounter trying to figure out what she did wrong. The only thing that stood out was the fact that she had initiated the sex, she had decided what they would do, and she had put Don in the submissive role.

His reaction reminded her of an episode on the ship when, during sex, she had playfully bound his wrists together with one of his ties. Immediately, his demeanor had changed from caring lover to serious and dominant with no regard for her. Tonight's activity had ended in much the same way. Don seemed to need the upper hand. *Something in his past has triggered this in him,* reasoned Beth to herself. *Someday, I'll find out what. We all have buttons that others can push which bring out a hidden side. Doesn't mean he's a bad person.*

Emerging from the shower, her good-natured husband had returned with no remnants of his temper or domineering persona. Taking it all in stride, Beth kissed her husband and then proceeded to take her turn in the bathroom.

The remainder of the evening centered on socializing, with the newlyweds enjoying the company of many others around the patio fire. On the drive home, Don surprised Beth by bringing up the subject of Beth relocating to Miami. Several times, Beth had attempted to discuss the matter, and all he would say was that he couldn't purchase another house until the estate sold, but he never made the effort to put the mansion on the market. Jumping at the opportunity to discuss it further, Beth said, "We're really excited to move. There is little left here for the boys and me now. Being with you is what matters, now that school will soon finish for the year. I think it's the perfect time to start house-hunting."

"When I get home, I'm going to start the process of selling the estate. I think it's important that we start our new life with a new home." That was just what Beth wanted to hear. Life was good, and it was going to get better.

Chapter 9

This time, saying goodbye to Don was easier. He was leaving to begin the first step to getting them all settled in Florida. He had to go if they were to make progress. Beth had things to do to keep her busy in Kendrick, as well. Her home needed to be listed on the market, and as she sought advice on choosing a realtor, she felt nostalgic for the first time. The house held many memories stuffed into each corner, wall and floor board. Leaving the house would be leaving a large chunk of her history. But then she thought of the future where so many new history-making opportunities awaited. She knew she could not root herself in the past forever; it wasn't fair to her or her sons. Even her friends understood and were cheering her on, and they were a tough sell.

After contacting a realtor, Beth arranged an appointment to do a walkthrough of the house; this would help Beth establish a selling price. The house would then be placed on MLS, Multiple Listing Service, within twenty-four hours. Now things were getting exciting!

Beth began the task of purging belongings in anticipation of the move. With Matt's clothes spread out all over the floor, Beth was engrossed in the task of separating items when she received a text from her friend Keely in New York City. Beth hadn't seen Keely, and the others from New York that she had met on a swinger's cruise, since last Thanksgiving. Keely had received the wedding picture and marriage announcement Beth had sent, and she was now inviting Beth and Don to New York. The text said that she, Larry, and Lori wanted to pay for a weekend luxury suite for the couple as a wedding gift. Beth was delighted! It would be the closest thing she and Don would have to a honeymoon. She would have to make arrangement for the kids, of course, and Don would have to take time from work, but it was only for a couple of nights. Beth immediately texted Keely, thanking her and her friends for the generous gift and promising to be in touch soon.

Beth's second communication was to her husband explaining the gift the New Yorkers had offered. As Don read the text, he immediately saw getting away as a big problem. Then it hit him. *Fuck! Why not?* he thought to himself. *If all goes according to plan, soon money won't be an issue. In a month or two, working may be only a shitty memory. So, why deny a free opportunity now?* Texting Beth back, he told her to pick the date and the time, and he would be there.

What? said Beth to herself, *This isn't the Don I know.* Thrilled with his response, she sent a message back to Keely. Now it would depend on the availability of childcare. But when she casually mentioned it to Cindy, her problem dissolved. Cindy offered to care for the boys any weekend Beth wanted. They would line up another kid-friendly weekend in Pittsburgh. Now it was just up to her to choose a date. The trip meant spending time with her husband, so she was anxious to go sooner than later. Beth's choice was sent via text to Keely, Don, and Cindy. Everyone approved. Keely wouldn't reveal the location of the suite until she and Don landed in NYC. All that she would say was that it was swanky!

Time waited for no one, and the New York weekend was there before Beth knew it. She had kept busy purging closets and drawers and the weekend away would be a welcome break. Her flight was in the late afternoon, and after work, Cindy would pick up the boys from Jess's house.

This time, Don's plane would arrive several hours before hers. She still didn't know any of the trip's details, but Keely assured her everything was taken care of. For a two-night stay, she didn't require checked baggage and immediately made her way toward the taxi stand as she had been instructed. That's when it began to make sense. Standing there was a gentleman she vaguely recognized, dressed in a chauffer's uniform holding a sign that said, "Lyons." Now, she knew where they were staying – in the penthouse at The Four Seasons. The same chauffeur had picked her up at Keely's apartment on her first New York visit.

At that time, Tom, who was also visiting New York, had felt it necessary to warn her about Don's character, insisting her boyfriend was not the upstanding citizen she thought he was. To have that conversation with Beth, Tom had sent the penthouse chauffeur to pick her up and bring her to The Four Seasons, so he could give her a piece of his mind. Beth had chalked it up to petty jealousy and had moved on. She was sure the driver was the same guy, meaning they would be living in opulence for the next few days with a Rolls Royce and driver at their disposal, free open bar, and heated toilet seats! She could get used to this kind of luxury, and with Don's money, she just might be able to.

The driver reached down, subtly removing the bag from her grip while escorting her to the waiting car. The darkly tinted windows kept its interior secret, but she knew her husband would be waiting in the backseat for some loving. As the back door was opened for her, she began, "Hi ba..." but was stopped in mid-sentence. There was no Don to hear her greeting. There was no one. In the time it took the driver to place her carry-on in the trunk, tears had sprung and were running down her cheeks.

"We are off to The Four Seasons, ma'am. Is there anywhere we need to stop along the way?" the driver politely asked.

"No, directly to The Four Seasons is fine," she replied dabbing her face with a tissue. As she settled down for the ride, she began to make excuses for Don. No doubt he would have candles lit and champagne chilling for her arrival. Yes, that was it. He was probably naked waiting to spoil her.

Beth excused the driver as she stepped into the elevator knowing it stopped directly in the penthouse foyer. The elevator doors opened to near darkness. *Mmm, this is a good start,* said Beth to herself. *This looks very cozy.* But the farther she walked into the apartment, the better she understood. The only light she could see was not from a candle or romantically dimmed chandelier but from a television screen mindlessly illuminating the deserted living room. With her heart beating fast, she knew she would find him waiting for her in the bedroom. And she was right. Don, still dressed, was fast asleep and snoring on top of the bed covers. The blinds and drapes were closed simulating the darkness of night. Beth paused at the doorway to admire her man. *He works so hard. No wonder he's tired,* she said to herself.

She sat gingerly on the edge of the bed and began to lovingly stroke his hair while brushing his lips with her own. When there was no reaction, she began patting him on the back while calling his name; that interrupted his rhythmical snoring, producing a quiet groan and a sigh. His eyes fluttered briefly, and without changing positions, he returned to a deep sleep. Now, she could detect a strong smell of liquor, and as her eyes adjusted to the room's light, she spotted a half empty bottle of Bourbon on the opposite bedside table. He wasn't tired – he was drunk and had passed out! No wonder he hadn't bothered to greet her at the airport.

This time, despite the deep hurt she was feeling, there were no tears. She was devastated, but anger overruled every other emotion. He could sleep it off, but she wasn't ready for bed yet. She would enjoy the elegant apartment tonight, even if it meant being spoiled alone.

Getting up from the bed, Beth unpacked what little she had brought. Keely had mentioned taking them to Quench, one of New York's finest sex clubs, on Saturday night. She had brought some of her expensive lingerie, a mini-dress suitable for the occasion, and a few other pieces of casual clothing. Once her things were put away, she washed up for bed, but because she hadn't brought anything to sleep in, she threw on the hotel's complementary, plush, white robe and made her way back to the living room. It was dark outside now, and the long, narrow windows beautifully showcased all Manhattan's lights.

Her stomach growled, and she remembered from Tom that all food was included with the suite and that the large menu would make her choices almost limitless. She was hungry, but it was clear she and Don would not be enjoying an intimate dinner together. She would have to take care of herself, so she made a call to room service. She placed her order, then wandered to the library to check out the wall of books. She had scanned each shelf, amazed at the variety of novels before her and had just sat down with a classic when a tuxedo-clad waiter appeared in the foyer. Her meal was tastefully presented on a rolling table boasting white linen and cut flowers. To her surprise, he did not leave the dishes on the cart but elegantly positioned a place setting on the opulent glass dining table.

Encouraging her to be seated, he gallantly pulled out her chair for her and then asked if she would enjoy wine with her dinner. With a nod of Beth's head, he scurried to the suite's extensive wine collection choosing a rare bottle of red that would pair well with her beef. Within seconds, he had the bottle uncorked and had poured just enough into a cut crystal glass for her to taste. The wine was warm and just sweet enough for her liking, and with a second nod, he filled her glass, dabbed the lip of the bottle with a white napkin, and silently disappeared with the empty cart.

For a moment, Beth had been able to forget that she was not alone in the suite, but now she could only look at the expanse of the empty table where Don's plate should be sitting. "Fuck him!" she said out loud as she cut into her perfectly prepared filet mignon.

Chapter 10

Don had awakened from his stupor to a dark room. He looked around, but the inky darkness would only confirm that he was lying on a bed. Realizing he was fully clothed, he slowly began to remember where he was. He had arrived at the penthouse via chauffeured limousine around dinnertime and had had a few drinks. While waiting for Beth's arrival, he had shut his phone off, relishing his time away from Miami. With each Bourbon, he felt more and more relaxed until he couldn't fight the alcohol any longer, and he had passed out.

Blinking until he could read the numbers on the bedside clock, he saw the display read 3:56. It could only mean it was the middle of the night. Attempting to sit up, he clumsily raised himself to a seated position while his head throbbed. Reaching behind him, he couldn't feel anyone else. By now, Beth should have been in bed with him. *What the hell? What was going on?* Now he had to pee, and when he turned on the bathroom light, two things happened. The bright fluorescent light made his head hurt, and he saw some of Beth's things on the counter. Finishing his business, he exited the bathroom to find his wife. He found her asleep in the second bedroom, but he had no desire to wake her up. He was in deep shit, and he knew it. *Fuck!* he said to himself.

Dawn was just breaking when Beth opened her eyes in the apartment's second suite. She didn't have to think hard to remember the previous night's events. Their first of only two nights together should have been full of fireside wine, cuddling, romantic sex and spooning all night long. The actual evening had been full of tears, wine to dull her grieving, and sleeping the night alone. She had attempted to sleep beside Don, but his snoring and her contempt for the man had driven her away. Now that she was fully awake, she knew she would not be able to fall back asleep.

She made her way to the attached opulent, marble bathroom to shower, sort out her feelings, and wonder how the day would play out. Her toiletries were in the other bathroom, so she would use those the hotel had provided instead. She had no desire to see Don anytime soon.

The shower was spectacular. She had never been in a shower so superb. It boasted a huge rain head directly above and shower heads on each wall, hitting her gloriously from all angles. The shower alone was almost worth the trip. Eventually, feeling waterlogged, Beth turned off the water and dried herself with the most luxurious, chocolate brown bath sheet she had ever felt. She turned her attention to the bathroom's array of gratis toiletries. Top of the line mousse, spray, lotions and other goodies sat waiting. Her long hair took much more time to fix than her short curls ever did, but she still loved their effect. Once she was satisfied with drying and curling her hair, she ventured out of the ensuite.

Attired only in the hotel's signature bathrobe, she headed toward the living room. Something smelled good. The dining room table was set for two with a large carafe of coffee and various condiments. Fluted, cut crystal glasses contained orange juice, and the luxurious linens, silver cutlery, and white china looked inviting. At the sound of Beth approaching, Don arose from the loveseat where he had been reading *The New York Times*. He rushed toward her expecting to gather her in his arms while offering a profuse apology. But before he could touch her, Beth held out her hand signaling him to stop in his tracks. Her body language meant business, and he did what he was told.

"Good morning, babe."

"Don't you good morning me, you piece of shit. How dare you ruin one of only two nights that we have together? I can't believe how insensitive you are. You couldn't wait for me to get here before you had a drink...or ten! First of all, I was so disappointed at the airport when the driver opened the limo door and you weren't inside. I thought you would have wanted to be with me as soon as I got off the plane." By now, the tears were falling freely as she continued. "Then, I was sure you'd be waiting for me here with a glass of champagne or maybe have a bubble bath drawn in celebration. But that didn't happen either. Instead, I found you drunk and passed out. Snoring so loudly I couldn't have slept with you even if I wanted to – which I didn't!"

Suddenly, Beth realized she was experiencing déjà vu. Each and every argument they had had; each time he had disappointed her; each private tear she had shed was always about the same thing – Don's selfishness. She had married an egocentric ass, and she told him so.

"I know, babe. I've let you down. I have been alone for so long, and even now that we're married, I'm still alone. I'm not used to having a wife and family to think about and put first. I'm still thinking, and obviously, acting like a bachelor. Once we live together like a real family, it will be different, I promise."

In her distress, it was difficult to process much, but what Don was saying had some truth to it. Maybe it was unrealistic for him to think like a husband and father when he was only able to fill those roles a day or two a month. As always, she gave him the benefit of the doubt and stepped forward into his arms.

"That's it, baby. Get it out, get it all out," encouraged Don as Beth sobbed on his shoulder. She let go of him in search of a tissue.

"You hungry, baby? I sure am."

"I'm sure you are. You missed dinner last night," said Beth sniffling, getting in one more little jab.

Ignoring her remark, Don said, "Once I heard you were up, I took the liberty of ordering breakfast. I had the waiter put it in the oven to keep warm. Are you ready for coffee and breakfast? Feeling better?"

"Yes, I'm fine, and I'd love to eat."

Beth and Don lingered over breakfast wondering what their day in New York City should look like. With the Rolls Royce and driver at their disposal, it was tempting to be chauffeured around the city sight – seeing and shopping. But then again, the newlyweds were seldom able to spend time alone together. Although Don was in favor of going out to a sports bar for cocktails, Beth nixed the idea, wanting instead to stay in the penthouse with her man. Don knew he was still treading on thin ice and was smart enough to go along with whatever Beth wanted.

After a relaxing breakfast, during which all unpleasant issues seemed to have been forgiven, Don lustily pulled off Beth's robe. The make-up sex had been wonderful right in front of the flickering fireplace, hovering far above Manhattan. They had ordered lunch, then dinner to be brought up to the penthouse where they enjoyed several more bottles of wine. Between meals, they had luxuriated in a jetted-tub, bubble bath, enjoying more cocktails while watching a terrible movie on the flat screen above the tub.

It was now time to get ready to go to Quench. The Rolls would first take them to pick up Keely and then to the club. Both Don and Beth were looking forward to experiencing something new. Keely had said that Larry and Lori were planning on being there, which made the evening sound even better.

Chapter 11

Beth was excited to see her New York friends again. Their wedding gift of a sumptuous penthouse was incredibly generous. Keely climbed into the Rolls Royce amid Beth's squeals of delight at seeing her friend. All three were excited to be together. The traffic slowed their journey down considerably, giving Beth and Keely time to visit and for the New York City visitors to soak up the huge city's lights and bustle, despite the advancing hour.

The limo driver pulled the car alongside the curb in a darkened section of Queens. It was clear the building was a converted warehouse, and if the whole thing was Quench, it was massive. As they entered, they could not see much. The lighting was dim with a soft glow. Just like Climax, there was a greeter ensuring the people entering were supposed to be there. There was no Barbie Doll greeter here, instead there was a Ken-like person, whose name tag read Kyle.

Once her eyes adjusted to the light, Beth could see Kyle much better. He was impeccably dressed in a black suit that matched his slicked-back hair. His face was clean shaven, making sure nothing got in the way of noticing his baby blue eyes. His perfectly shaped, white teeth had to have been expensive, and who knew how many hours he had spent working on his tan? He stood well over six feet tall, and his broad shoulders, thick neck, and wide chest indicated the gym was his best friend. All in all, he was luscious. After politely asking them to hand over their electronic devices, Kyle wished them all a good evening checking off their names from his extensive guest list.

The group walked through the foyer and into a massive open space that resembled a large, hotel lobby. The walls were painted a dark red, and all the furniture and lamps looked like antiques from another century; making Beth think of the burlesque era. A pretty, fifty-something woman stood up from her Louis XIV desk as she saw the guests approaching.

"Rosanna, good evening, how are you?" greeted Keely, as she kissed the woman on both cheeks.

"Keely, my love. So nice to see you. You've brought guests."

"Yes, this is Beth and Don, friends of mine from out of town. Rosanna and her friend, Maggie, are the club owners."

"Good to meet you Beth, Don," said Rosanna, as she warmly shook both their hands.

"Good to meet you, too," said Beth.

"Why don't you three head to the bar and grab a cocktail? Then I can give you all the grand tour."

As they took Rosanna up on her suggestion, Beth asked Keely, "How does one end up owning a swingers' club in New York City?"

"Well, Rosanna is Canadian-born, married to a retired NHL player, so they moved around a lot with his hockey career. Oliver's last trade was to a New York team, and they loved the city so much, they decided to stay. Rosanna decided it was her turn to work after years of raising kids and following Oliver around in his hockey career, so she looked for a business opportunity and found this warehouse. They met Maggie when they were looking for investment advice after Oliver retired. Maggie worked on Wall Street, and they hired her to do some financial planning for them. The two women hit it off and became friends. At first, Maggie was a silent partner in Rosanna's business, but after a few years of seeing how much fun Rosanna was having, she quit her finance job and began working here full time. Neither of them are swingers, but they obviously endorse the lifestyle and work hard to make this a safe, pleasurable experience for their members and guests.

"Wow! That's quite a story," said Beth. "That answers my question. You haven't been to the club in Kendrick but, I assure you, it's nothing like this. Does Quench take up the whole building?"

"No, I think maybe half to two thirds. It seems I remember being told there are about forty playrooms on three levels. There is a bar on each floor."

"In Kendrick, there is dinner served each evening, for a fee, if people want."

"There are no meals offered here, just hors d'oeuvres. You'll see some canapés and snacks near each of the bars. Maggie oversees the food and bar service of the club. When she's here, you'll often see her bartending – she likes to interact with the patrons. Rosanna fills more of the hostess role. She gets to know the members, too, in a much different way. She keeps a database of members' preferences, so she can reserve the appropriate room for them."

"What do you mean the right room?"

"Many of the playrooms are themed taking into account different fetishes or ambiances. For example, there is a naughty nurse room, a foot fetish room, and an S & M room, among others. Some rooms have costumes, toys, and props, or people can bring their own. Some guests come dressed in costume."

Unlike Kendrick, patrons' alcohol was not stored at the club. The establishment was run like a country club. Each year, members were charged a joining fee and expected to put down twenty-five thousand dollars. Members had tabs, and all charges were simply deducted from the balance. Keely instructed the bartender to mix drinks for her and her friends, placing the amount on her tab. As they strolled away from the bar with drinks in hand, Keely reminded them that discretion was very important. Members of Quench included musicians, movie stars, television personalities, politicians, right on down to soccer moms. There were written policies for members and their guests but also unwritten ones. No one was to ask for autographs, and no photos were to be taken.

"Is that why we had to give up our cell phones?" asked Don.

"Yes," answered Keely, "that's exactly why. It's too easy, in a place like this, for someone to take a picture of a celebrity or public figure and post it on social media or blackmail one of the guests with it. So, they try to eliminate as much risk as possible, hopefully allowing all guests to relax."

"Yep, we are certainly not in Kendrick anymore," chuckled Beth.

"Even in Miami there are no strict rules like this," said Don.

"But your clubs aren't full of celebrities," reasoned Keely.

They turned to see Rosanna walking toward them. She was an elegant-looking lady in her fifties. Her chestnut brown hair was styled short with the odd gray hair shimmering in the light. The royal blue cocktail dress accentuated her trim figure. She smiled broadly as she approached them, causing the appearance of tiny wrinkles beside each eye. Beth could already tell she would like this woman. She seemed kindly and self-assured, someone who would make a good friend.

Beginning the tour, Rosanna reiterated some of the house rules that Keely had already alluded to. She explained the partnership she and Maggie had and introduced the trio to her partner who was slinging drinks behind the second-floor bar.

Maggie was as outgoing as one could be. Her huge smile was as big as her personality, and it was clear there was mutual admiration and respect, not to mention loads of fun between the two owners. Both women made it clear that their mission was to provide a clean, safe private club for those who enjoyed the alternative lifestyle. Maggie made sure to point out the unique bar menu that hung on the wall.

QUENCH - DRINK LIST*
(GRAB A...)   (GET SOME...)
COCK---TAILS

NAME	INGREDIENTS
MISTRESS MAGGIE'S MELON MASH (SMOOTH AND LUSCIOUS)	WATERMELON VODKA, MANGO-PINEAPPLE VODKA, FRESCA, SPLASH OF GRENADINE
ROSANNA'S BANANA LEG SPLIT (STIFF AND HARD)	CRÈME DE BANANA IRISH CREAM
SIX FEET UNDER (UNDER THE COVERS, THAT IS)	LEMON & MELON VODKA, COCONUT RUM, SWEET 'N SOUR MIX, 7-UP
CHERRY POPPER (SIP IT SLOW AND EASY)	CHERRY SCHNAPPS, 7-UP, A CHERRY
JUICY FRUIT COCKTAIL (GAY FRIEND FAVORITE)	MELON & PEACH LIQUEUR, RAINBOW SHERBET VODKA, PINEAPPLE JUICE
S'MORE PLEASE (WHO DOESN'T WANT MORE?)	S'MORE VODKA, IRISH CREAM, CHOCOLATE LIQUEUR
JOHN JUAN (SMOOTH, ENDS WITH A BANG)	ROOT BEER VODKA, VANILLA LIQUEUR, CREAM
RIMMER (GLORIOUSLY KINKY)	BACON INFUSED RYE, SWEET VERMOUTH, BITTERS, BACON DIPPED IN CHOC & SEA SALT
HOT ASS (IN MORE WAYS THAN ONE)	FIRE PUNCHER VODKA, HOT SAUCE, JALAPENO PEPPER
MORAN'S PURPLE PASSION (BRINGS OUT YOUR PASSION)	VODKA, PINEAPPLE, ORANGE AND GRAPE JUICE, LIME, A CHERRY
TEA BAGGER (LIFT IT AND LAP IT)	FRUIT LOOPS VODKA, ICED TEA
JIZZ FIZZ (FOAMY FIZZ SLIPS RIGHT DOWN)	VODKA, WHITE RUM, IRISH CREAM

PLEASE DRINK RESPONSIBLY

<u>QUENCH - DRINK LIST*</u>
<u>MARTINIS</u>

<u>NAME</u>	<u>INGREDIENTS</u>
THE LIFESTYLE SIGNATURE MARTINI (DARE TO SHARE)	GOLDSCHLAGGER SCHNAPPS, KRUG CHAMPAGNE
DIRTY MARTINI (THE ORIGINAL RECIPE)	GIN, DRY VERMOUTH, OLIVE JUICE, OLIVE
BIRTHDAY SUIT MARTINI (LOOKS GOOD ON EVERYBODY)	BIRTHDAY CAKE VODKA, CHOC LIQUEUR, AMARETTO, ½ & ½
KNOTTY MARTINI (IN HONOR OF OUR KNOT MASTER)	FIREWEED VODKA, VIOLETTE LIQUEUR, GRAPE JUICE
BLOW ME MARTINI (YUMMY, YUMMY)	BUBBLE GUM VODKA, SOUR WATERMELON, LEMONADE, BLOW POP
HIT THE HOLE MARTINI (TAKE CAREFUL AIM)	GLAZED DONUT VODKA, CRÈME DE CACAO, VANILLA SYRUP, CREAM

PLEASE DRINK RESPONSIBLY

<u>NON-ALCOHOLIC</u>

<u>NAME</u>	<u>INGREDIENTS</u>
BEND OVER SHIRLEY (KIND OF SPEAKS FOR ITSELF)	RASPBERRY SODA, LEMON-LIME SODA, GRENADINE
VIRGIN MARY (REALLY???)	GRAPE JUICE, SPRITE

SELECTION OF JUICES AND SODAS

They left Maggie pouring drinks and good-naturedly ribbing an approaching couple while Rosanna took the group to the third floor.

Most of the playrooms in Kendrick and Miami were very stark in nature. Beds were adorned with only a fitted bottom sheet. Other than a sex chair or swing, the only other difference between rooms was the color of paint on the walls and carpet on the floor. Quench was altogether different. Many of the rooms were decorated with either a fetish in mind or a particular theme. They saw a room that had dozens of pairs of shoes, framed pictures of feet on the walls, and a basin and towels sat nearby for a luxurious foot bath. Obviously, this was the foot fetish room.

There was the naughty nurse room complete with medical equipment including a TENS unit. Nurses' uniforms, white lab coats and patient gowns hung ready for those who wanted to role play. There was also the naughty school girl room and the cowboy room, which was decorated with antique furniture and accessories from the 1800s. The Karma Sutra room had no bed; the baby room featured a large crib, adult diapers, bonnets and bottles. A strip-tease room featured a small stage with a stripper pole, and the Furries's room boasted a closet full of furry, animal costumes. Rosanna made sure her group understood that the club owned multiples of each costume in various sizes. Once a costume was worn, it was sent out to be dry cleaned, assuring the club's cleanliness.

The last room was unique indeed. It was built in a portion of the first floor and could be viewed from all four sides through large picture windows. It was called the Japanese Knot Room. The space was not large, but what space there was, was covered in aromatic cedar. The raised platform in the center of the room had large hooks screwed into the ceiling trusses. Off to one side were a multitude of carefully coiled hemp ropes of various thicknesses and lengths.

"Is this an S & M room?" asked Don.

"No, not quite," answered Rosanna. "We may be the only club on the planet to boast a room like this. It was built to the exact specifications of a Japanese knot master named Kim Ren."

Few things at a sex club were considered truly unique or out of the ordinary. With the array of members and guests, along with their different sexual preferences and idiosyncrasies, as long as it was legal and consensual, it had likely been tried or at least witnessed, especially in New York City. That's why when talk among the members circled around a Japanese knot master at Quench, people were curious, to say the least.

Chapter 12

It took years to reach the level of master, much like the time and practice it took to become a martial arts master or a Sumo wrestler. The major difference was that these experts were often on public display while the knot master displayed his talents in a more private venue. Kim Ren, an American citizen had spent the last twenty years in Japan pursuing his business career. He had fallen in love with the Japanese way of life, its customs and traditions, and only came to the States when necessary. But when he did, he made time in his schedule to indulge himself at Quench. He had no relationship partner. He liked it that way – he was one of a kind in many ways, all of which were appreciated by women. In the sexual world, Kim had a reputation, and any woman who had witnessed his flawless techniques lined up to be his lady for the night.

Tonight, Kim was still in Japan. He was on his way to the pink light district. His destination was not a drab building with illegal prostitutes under the rule of a *mama-san.* Rather, Kim, considered a high-class patron, would walk into a handsome building, its interior paneled with expensive pecan and walnut: the bar inside always well-stocked. Kim frequented this business several nights a week after long days at work.

He was now near the building that was so familiar to him. It was dark and the street was quiet. There were no bright neon signs or cafes spilling tables and chairs out onto the sidewalk. The street was void of all traffic. With no headlights, the only source of light was a wooden pole, slightly leaning toward the road, with a street light perched near the top; the light so dim, it barely cast a shadow as he walked beneath it. The click, click of his highly-polished black leather shoes hit the sidewalk with authority. He knew where he was going and the undesirable neighborhood did not make him uneasy.

Kim stepped into the establishment with briefcase in hand. Without a word, the discreet bartender recognized him and set up his drink before he had time to settle into a chair. Winding down and sipping a couple of drinks always preceded his female encounters. Once relaxed, with business forgotten, Kim bowed to the bartender and then walked through an unmarked door into the posh locker room where regulars were given the run of the area and its amenities. Kim wasted no time undressing, perfectly folding his suit, shirt, tie, underwear and socks and then laying them on the bench in front of his locker.

As he was putting on a towel, his clothing was discreetly whisked away for cleaning and pressing. His first stop was the steam room. Then he would be ushered into a private massage room with his two favorite *geisha* girls. Although they wore no traditional makeup or kimonos, their mandate was the same as the geishas of centuries ago, to please their man. Following his steam session, the first order of business was a sensual sponge bath given simultaneously by both women. Expensive lanolin soap was applied to sponges harvested from the Japanese Sea. He was well-known by his girls, and they knew exactly what he liked and how he liked it. There was not a word spoken; there was no need. The lights were dim. The aroma of beeswax permeated the air as burning candles added to the atmosphere. As the girls dried Kim with soft, white, pre-warmed towels, he knew to transfer over to the massage table. Rare emu oil was used as both women began the sensual massage.

They were both naked. There was no pretense as to why they were there and what their role was. The women were of typical Japanese build, very slender with small frames, looking younger than their years. Their breasts were small with their nipples and areolas looking disproportionately large. The black pubic hair remained intact, all part of this particular sexual culture.

The massage changed from his back to his front. The girls were pleased with his erection, and he discreetly motioned to the girl he had chosen to penetrate. With a minimum of sound, Kim experienced his orgasm, then was given time to recoup before both women once again cleansed him with soap and water. The sequence of events never changed just as the girls never changed. They were there to please him, and over time they developed the strict ritual that made Kim feel powerful and pampered.

Mr. Ren was feeling cleansed in all ways. With the private geisha house behind him, the limo sped toward Narita International Airport. He was expected in New York City within forty-eight hours to discuss business. His only baggage was his briefcase. He didn't need any luggage for he maintained a small, stark apartment in Manhattan, which contained a duplicate of his Tokyo wardrobe and toiletries. Ren was an intense man of strict demeanor. Whether in New York or Tokyo his schedule changed as little as possible.

He was a loner, an observer, not interested in getting to know anyone and always on guard, keeping others from knowing him. He followed a strict code of honor, expecting respect from others and giving respect back, with no patience for those who did not respect man and nature. If asked for one word to describe himself, Kim Ren would immediately, sternly, and confidently answer "disciplined." It would, therefore, surprise no one that he had mastered several martial arts and was an expert with many kinds of weaponry from Samurai swords to military grade rifles.

Back at Quench, Rosanna continued to tour the guests.

"That sounds very interesting," said Beth as she looked at Don.

"Not everyone is into getting tied up," said Don flatly.

"It's so much more than that," said Rosanna, "You should come back when Mr. Ren is here and see for yourself."

"Thank you so much for the tour Rosanna," said Beth. "We know you are busy, and we are excited to try out one of your rooms."

Rosanna ended the tour while emphasizing the cleanliness of the club and the health of its patrons and encouraging the use of condoms. As she wrapped up the tour, she couldn't emphasize strongly enough the privacy and discretion that each guest was assured, stating it was the cornerstone of their business. After the formalities, Rosanna bid them a great evening.

"Enjoy!" said Rosanna with a smirk, as she turned to speak to one of her workers.

"Let's try one of those drink specials and decide what we want to do," suggested Beth.

"Great idea," said Don while steering Beth to the bar on the third floor. "What looks good to you, honey?" asked Don.

"I think I will try Maggie's Melon Mash."

"And I will have a John Juan," laughed Don.

The bartender made his way over to Beth and Don and took their orders, charging them to Keeley as she had previously permitted. He deftly mixed and poured Beth's melon flavored cocktail as well as Don's root beer flavored drink.

Beth took a sip and said, "So, the same rules apply here, right? No penetration except with each other."

"Of course, babe."

"What room do you want to try?" asked Beth.

"I'm not sure I want to try any of them quite yet, to be honest," said Don.

"Why? What's wrong?"

"I just want to try out a few drinks and let you hang out with Keely. I know how much you've missed her."

"Well, that's true, but I want to show off my husband here," pouted Beth.

"You will, honey. Go have fun. I'll be right here when you're done." Standing up as if to dismiss her, Don kissed Beth's lips lightly and winked.

"Okay, I'll go find Keely," replied Beth.

Don sat back down and ordered another drink. He drank it quickly, then hurried to the room that had most interested him on Rosanna's tour. He had hoped the woman he saw was still there and ready for more action.

Beth had no trouble finding Keely. She was chatting with Maggie at the Quench bar on the second floor.

"Hey, where's Don?" asked Keely.

"My wonderful husband told me to have some girl fun first," lied Beth.

Maggie laughed, throwing her head back slightly as she did. Her full, pink lips parted showing off her straight, white teeth. She tossed her long blonde hair over her shoulder, and her green eyes gleamed when she looked directly at Keely and asked, "Are you going to initiate this girl in full Quench style, or are you going to ease her in?"

"Hmm, you know where I want to take her."

"Go for it," replied Maggie before she turned to a group of men who were approaching the bar.

"Should I be worried?" giggled Beth.

"Come on. We're going down to the first floor."

Beth followed Keely down the wide carpeted staircase and toward the right hallway. Without hesitation, Keely chose the third doorway on the left. She pushed open the heavy oak door and held it for Beth to enter. Beth's eyes, needing to adjust to the dimly lit room, opened wide to take in her surroundings. She looked overhead at three, low hung hammered iron chandeliers. Each was suspended by four, antique chains, and held dozens of flameless candles. On each wall hung black metal torches, also lit by large, flickering, flameless bulbs. The lighting danced across deep crimson walls, allowing for distorted shadowing and an eerie feel.

"Oh, Lord," breathed Beth. Keely had chosen the Medieval Torture Room. Beth could only stare at the rectangular, wooden table in the center of the room. On either end of the table were rollers with a ratchet and handle device. There were ropes attached to each roller with ankle and wrist restraints at the end of each rope.

Beth looked to Keely, who smiled and said, "The Rack. Don't worry – the pulleys don't tighten too much, and the shackles loosely restrain you. And over there is the Chair of Torture. It's really just a sex chair. Those spike are actually made of stiff rubber and kind of massage you all over when you sit in it."

"And what about him?" asked Beth, pointing to the masked man who walked out of the shadows from the corner of the room.

"He's the Executioner. He monitors the activities and is also a skilled dominator for those who want a little pain with their pleasure."

Beth eyed the tall, muscular mystery man wearing a short, black leather loin cloth, knee-high leather boots, and spiked, black leather gloves that flared at each wrist. His torso was clothed in leather chains that crisscrossed him front and back. His head and neck were covered by a black fabric hood with cut-outs for his deep brown eyes and unsmiling mouth. He held a long-handled ax in front of him completing his somewhat threatening appearance.

"Let me show you his table of goodies," teased Keely.

Beth obediently followed Keely to the far end of the room where a red, velvet-lined table abutted the wall. Keely lightly touched each item and said, "Rubber nipple pinchers, riding crop, flagellated whip, cock stock..."

"Wait," interrupted Beth, "a cock stock?"

"Yeah. You know, like a cock cage, or chastity device. See? It even has a padlock," laughed Keely holding it in front of Beth's nose. "There's a rubber paddle, mouth gags, blindfold. Well, you get the picture – lots of variety. And all devices are soaked in antiseptic between each use."

"Some of those items aren't exactly medieval," observed Beth.

"Well, there are some overtones from the BDSM room, for sure!" laughed Keely.

Beth wandered away from the table and took a closer look at the art hanging on the walls. Hand-drawn illustrations of how actual torture devices from the Medieval Age were used, hung from wide, mahogany frames. *Hard to believe any guy could get an erection in this room*, thought Beth.

Keely walked up behind Beth, wrapping her arms across Beth's breasts in a warm embrace. Beth turned and hungrily sought Keely's warm lips and mouth with her own. Darting her tongue inside Keely's mouth, she tasted the cinnamon from the Quench champagne martini still lingering inside. Pressing her hands firmly against Beth's breasts, she kneaded them through her silk blouse and lace brassiere. Beth moaned and found Keely's breasts while continuing the assault on her mouth. Keely wasted no time grasping the hem of Beth's blouse and pulling it up over her head. She then grasped Beth by her hips and guided her to the rack. She continued kissing her deeply before pulling down Beth's skirt to the floor.

Beth grabbed the edge of the table and hoisted herself up until she was sitting with her legs hanging over the side. Keely gently nudged Beth so that she was lying lengthwise on the table. Moving to the head of the rack, Keely reached down and, pulling both of Beth's arms, slipped both wrists into the restraints.

Keely moved around the side of the table and climbed on, astride Beth. She ran the palms of her hands up Beth's torso and slipped her fingers under the cups of Beth's bra. Her fingers found Beth's erect nipples and rolled them between the thumb and index finger of each hand.

Beth moaned and said, "Suck them."

Keely pushed Beth's bra up over her breasts, freeing them from captivity. She dropped her wet mouth over one nipple and sucked hard while swirling her tongue over its peak. Her hand rubbed firmly across Beth's other nipple.

"Ahh," said Beth as she arched her back toward Keely, driving her breast further into Keely's mouth.

Sliding down the table and Beth's legs, Keely hooked

her fingers under the top of Beth's lacy black thong and slowly slid it downward, throwing it to the floor. Beth opened her legs, while Keely got off the table and slid Beth's ankles into each restraint. She turned the handle of the roller, slightly tightening the ropes, and spreading Beth even more.

Beth writhed on the table, aching for Keely to use her tongue between her legs.

"Lick my pussy. Please, lick my pussy!" shouted Beth.

Ignoring Beth's pleas, Keely walked over to the executioner's table and picked up the cat-o-nine tail whip. Beth's eyes followed her but offered no objection, as Keely approached her, whip in hand and stood at the foot of the table. Taking the whip, Keely drew her arm back slightly and slapped Beth's genitals with a quick snap of her wrist. The leather tails lightly slapped her shaved labia, causing a light pink to spread across both lips. Keely immediately bent forward and delivered light kisses where she had just struck.

"Again," urged Beth.

Keely struck Beth again, this time with a fraction more force, never taking her eyes off Beth's face. She didn't want to hurt or scare her, but seeing only pleasure on Beth's face, she whipped her again several more times.

Dropping the whip, Keely stretched herself forward until she could easily reach Beth's pussy. She lightly licked up and down each labia, then parted Beth's burning lips with the fingers of her left hand. Keely ran her tongue over Beth's clitoris in a circular motion until the tissue swelled. She licked downward to the opening of Beth's vagina and lapped at it like a greedy kitten with a bowl of milk.

Beth writhed on the table pulling at her restraints but not wanting to be free. She was a moving target for Keely, who had to latch her mouth firmly over Beth's womanhood while the fingers of her right hand stroked Beth's pussy on the inside. She continued to suck her vaginal opening while darting her tongue inside and back up to the clitoral peak. It was not long before Beth yelled out, "I'm cuming! I'm cuming!"

Keely stayed focused and continued to drink Beth's juices until Beth relaxed and went limp on the table.

Don walked through the doorway of the infant room. He was not interested in the adult size playpen, changing table, or rocking chair; nor the rattles, talcum powder, baby bottles or diapers. His eyes were locked on the beautiful ebony skinned woman kneeling on the carpeted floor in the corner of the room. Her long, black hair hung in loose curls around her small shoulders. Her arms and legs were lean and her belly was flat down to her neatly trimmed pubic area. Her large breasts, with dark brown areola and nipples, were engorged with milk that he could see dripping from one nipple. Attached to her other breast was a man sitting on his knees before her, suckling, making loud gulping sounds.

"You are gorgeous," breathed Don, as he took in her beautiful, heart-shaped face. Her hazel eyes were framed by long, curled, sooty lashes, and her broad nose was perched above full lips stained in red.

"You're hot, too," she said with a slight curl of her lips.

"Get lost," she said to her companion as she unlatched him from her somewhat deflated breast.

He got off the floor, wiping his mouth and, without a word, walked past Don, and closed the baby gate door behind him.

"So, do you need a mommy tonight?" teased his

playmate.

"I want to suck your tit and fuck your pussy if that's what Mommy wants," said Don as he started unbuttoning his dress shirt.

She answered him by sitting back with her knees bent, leaning on her arms posed straight behind her. Watching Don strip, she opened and closed her knees slowly and rhythmically, giving him a peek at the mysterious dark triangle between her legs.

Don playfully crawled to her, pushed her legs wide apart, and sat between her knees. He placed his hands on either side of her face and kissed her mouth, darting his tongue around until it clashed with her own. She eagerly returned his kisses, and sank back on the carpet, pulling Don down on top of her as she did. His mouth slid from the warmth of her mouth to the erect, leaking nipple of her right breast.

He took her nipple and areola into his mouth, clamped down and sucked. Warm breast milk gushed forth, and Don could barely keep up with the flow. He swallowed and sucked until her breast was empty.

Fully aroused, he grabbed his cock, quickly rolling down his condom and pushed inside her dark, beckoning cavern. She wrapped her legs around Don pulling him in and pushing him away to match his rhythm.

"Oh, God," moaned Don.

He furiously battered her juicy snatch with his throbbing pole. He had been so totally turned on by sucking her lactating breasts that he thought he might cum before he could ever fuck her. She bucked her pelvis and pulled Don deeper and deeper into her depths; her mouth sought his again and sucked on his tongue until Don pulled his mouth from her and said, "I'm going to cum!"

"Go, baby. That's the way to fuck me."

Hearing those words, Don released his load and threw his head back as he tried to catch his breath. He smiled down at her and said, "That was incredible. Thank you."

"Anytime, baby. I have been able to keep my milk flowing for almost a year now," she said proudly.

Don got up, pulled the condom off, and threw it into the plastic lined diaper pail. Grabbing a huge cloth diaper, he wiped his cock off and quickly redressed.

"What's your hurry?" she asked quizzically.

"I've got a wife who will be looking for me soon," Don said with a hint of disgust in his voice. "Gotta go."

Beth and Keely were in the hallway heading back to the second-floor bar when they ran into Lori and Larry.

"Hey, where are you two headed?" asked Keely.

"Larry is in the mood for a little S & M," laughed Lori.

"Oh, and you're not?" teased Larry.

"We'll see," teased Lori right back.

"Care to join us?" Lori directed to Keely and Beth.

Beth answered first, and said, "I'm sure Don is wondering where I am, and I could use another drink."

"Ditto," replied Keely. "But I'll catch up with you in a little."

"See you later, then," smiled Lori as she clasped Larry's hand in her own and walked down the flight of stairs to the first floor.

"They really have a great marriage, don't they?" Beth asked Keely.

"They do. Sometimes I am envious. I want a husband and maybe children someday."

"I don't know what I would do without my kids," said Beth thoughtfully, suddenly missing her boys and taking her mind far from the club and sex.

"So, do you have time for Maggie to make us a quick drink? Or do you need to hunt your hubby down?" asked Keely, a smile tugging at the corners of her mouth.

"Let him hunt me down. I want another drink. He will find me."

Beth and Keely found the last two empty bar stools, and Keely ordered two of the Quench signature champagne drinks. They bantered with Maggie, the other bartender, and then Rosanna, who stopped to drink a quick glass of ice water. Beth was enjoying the conversation so much that she and Keely had another champagne.

Maggie and Rosanna's laughter quickly came to a halt when the medical emergency alarm went off. It was a silent alarm that the employees recognized by the flashing strobe lights that were strategically placed near the ceiling on all the walls of the club. There were certain sequences that represented different type of emergencies. The emergency system was automatically connected to 911 so that the police and ambulance would already be alerted and dispatched. An attendant ran up to Rosanna and whispered into her ear. Immediately, Rosanna turned to her partner and said, "Apparent heart attack, Maggie. First floor," as she ran toward the stairway with her partner at her heels.

Keely looked to Beth and said, "You're a nurse. Let's go!"

Keely and Beth ran down the steps in hot pursuit of the club owners. They saw the commotion in the hallway outside one of the playrooms, and Beth pushed her way through the growing crowd.

Inside the S & M playroom, Beth saw Maggie kneeling beside Larry, who was lying on a wide massage table. She was counting out loud as she delivered chest compressions while Rosanna stood at the head of the table, blowing air into Larry's mouth through a face shield.

"Oh, God!" said Beth, turning and hoping that Keely hadn't entered the room.

"Larry!" screamed Keely as she searched the room for Lori.

Lori, sobbing loudly, was being escorted from the room by the Dominatrix. Keely ran up to Lori pushing the other woman from her friend. Beth, seeing that Maggie and Rosanna knew what they were doing, joined Keely and left the room to console Lori.

Rosanna yelled to the Dominatrix, "Get that fucking cage off his penis!"

The Dominatrix grabbed the key and fumbled with the padlock. Once the locked was removed, she had difficulty removing the plastic cage due to how incredibly swollen and engorged Larry's penis was.

The paramedics rushed in, pushing a gurney, followed by the police. Not wanting to be recognized, the crowd quickly dispersed with the arrival of the medical personnel and law enforcement officers. Two medics took over CPR and control of the automated heart defibrillator, while the third paramedic interviewed Lori.

How much alcohol? What medications was he taking? Any drug use tonight? What medical problems did he have? Lori had trouble concentrating on the questions she was asked, but with the help of Keely, she was able to inform the paramedic that Larry had consumed five alcoholic drinks and was taking blood pressure and cholesterol medications. She also mentioned sheepishly that her husband had recently taken Viagra with Ecstasy.

After the IV was inserted into Larry's arm, he was

transferred onto the gurney while CPR continued out to the ambulance. Lori and Keely followed the paramedics to the front entrance, and Lori got into one of the police cars to follow the ambulance to the hospital.

Don approached Beth and Keely and asked, "What the hell is going on?"

"Where have you been, Don? Dear God! Larry had a cardiac arrest, and the paramedics just took him," shouted Beth.

"I've been looking for you, damn it!" stammered Don.

"I have to go. I'm going to take Lori and Larry's car back to their place. Beth, are you okay to follow me and bring my car?" asked Keely.

"Sure, we can," said Beth.

"I'll do the driving. I haven't had much to drink," said Don. *Alcohol, that is.*

Although Beth had had plenty of questions brewing for Don about his whereabouts at Quench, all was now forgotten. The couple sat in silence as the two of them tried to process what had just taken place and while Don concentrated on keeping Keely in sight. With Larry's car safely parked in the driveway, Keely got behind the wheel of her car while Don moved to the backseat.

"I want to go to the hospital," said Keely, not asking but telling her passengers.

"Yes, of course," replied Beth. "Oh, God, I hope he's okay."

"He just has to be," said Keely with quivering lips.

Keely hastily parked the car, and the three of them half walked, half ran to the emergency entrance. The automatic sliding doors opened wide welcoming them to a distinctly unfamiliar world. The bright lights, smells, hustling personnel and sounds were foreign to them all including Beth. It was vastly different when in a hospital for personal medical reasons. After announcing who they were looking for, the nurse at the desk encouraged them to take a seat. Larry was being attended to, and his wife was with him. Other than that, the nurse had no further progress report.

The friends had sat nervously at first, watching every person who came and went from the ER, hoping they had some news. But after a couple of hours, they began to relax as fatigue took over from nervous energy. Don was asleep in the chair, his head cocked to one side held up by his hand; Beth flipped mindlessly through a magazine while Keely was watching the sun come up. Then Keely saw Lori walking toward them. She instantly stood up and ran to her, throwing her arms around her friend.

The sudden movement woke up Don, and Beth noticed, too. Lori suddenly went limp in Keely's arms. It was as if she had remained stoic on her own, but now she would eagerly share her shock and horror with her good friends. Keely helped her over to a chair while Lori sobbed.

The trio tried not to pepper her with too many questions. Clearly, she was still in shock and totally exhausted. They learned Larry had survived so far and was resting in Cardiac ICU. The staff had encouraged her to go home and get some rest with the assurance that they would call her if there were any change in his condition. Keely decided to stay with Lori while Beth and Don went back to The Four Seasons.

By the time Beth and Don boarded their planes home, Larry was doing much better. They had gone to see him and were amazed at how good he had looked. The doctors had inserted a stent into a blocked artery and Larry would require some cardiac rehab, but all in all, it could have been much worse. His lifestyle would need a shake-up. He was instructed to change his diet, exercise routine, and decrease his stress level, meaning he was to work normal business hours at the bakery. Beth gave him a kiss and a good long squeeze as she said goodbye. She also informed him that New York City was interesting enough and that in the future she would appreciate it if he didn't bother with manufacturing added excitement just to spice things up for her. Don laughed in agreement with Beth's sentiment and gave his friend a hug and a handshake on the way to the airport.

The weekend in New York City ended far too quickly for Beth. Having to say goodbye to her husband, friends, and the city itself was depressing. Thankfully, Larry was progressing well. She promised to stay in close touch with Lori, Larry, and Keely.

The only bright spot was Don promising to come to Kendrick one last time to help her pack up the house when it sold. Beth had plenty to do upon her return home. Besides continuing to purge her belongings in preparation for the move, she was determined to begin the paperwork to legally change her name on various documents and speak to Don's bank in Miami, as well as her financial advisor and banker in Kendrick. Her goal was to get her name on Don's bank accounts in Miami, so she could easily transfer her checking and savings accounts. She also wanted to liquidate much of her portfolio in preparation for buying a new estate in Florida. She would need a substantial amount of money on hand for a down payment.

Once that was done, the balance of her portfolio would be set up in a joint mutual fund account with Don's financial advisor. This was the part of marriage that she didn't like. The legal and financial paperwork was boring and at times difficult to understand. Luckily, she had Don to help her.

In the midst of going to a thrift store to donate several bags and boxes of goods, Beth received a text from Jack and Cindy inviting her and the boys over for dinner. Following a great meal, with the boys playing in the backyard, Jack and Cindy asked Beth for an update on Larry. Then they revealed the true reason for the invitation. They had heard from Jess that Beth needed to head to Miami to look for a new home and to finalize some financial paperwork.

"Heard from Jess that you need to get to Miami soon."

"Yes, it seems there are a few things I need to take care of before we can make the move, and the sooner I get some of the paperwork done, the better. We also really need to start looking for a new home, and Don keeps saying he is too busy, so I guess I will take the bull by the horns and start looking."

"We have a proposition for you which might make things a little simpler."

"Oh, really? What?"

"You already know that we get along great with the boys, and we love them as if they were our own. We were wondering while you have to fly to and from Miami if Jack and I might keep the boys for you. I mean, it would obviously be temporary – just until you find a house and make the move."

"You mean, keep them full time for a month or two?"

"Yes, something like that. You could sign over temporary guardianship, so we could have medical power of attorney and signing authority at their school should we need it," explained Cindy.

"Oh, my gosh – I don't know. It seems like a big step."

"It's actually a very simple process, and we know how stressed you are about organizing your life and theirs in Miami. We thought it would help you out and provide stability for the kids."

"I don't know, guys. I'll have to think about it and talk to Don."

"That's fine, Beth. Take your time. Just know we are always here for you."

Beth opened the back door to call the boys in to go home. While doing so, she couldn't help but notice a newly built structure in the Ward's backyard. It was a beautiful, new tree house, but somehow Jack and Cindy didn't seem like the tree climbing type.

Once home, after bath time, Beth tucked them into bed. After her shower, she sat down with her tablet. She had a sense of uneasiness about the Ward's offer, but could not pinpoint why. It was generous and made perfect sense, so why was she feeling hesitant about accepting it? She needed to talk it over with Don. He would help her with her decision.

Chapter 13

The boys and their gear, a full car load, had been lovingly dropped off at Jack and Cindy's home. Now, Beth was sitting at 33,000 feet on her way to Miami to start house-hunting, not just house-hunting but mansion hunting! She knew funding it, at least at first, would be her financial responsibility as much of Don's money was tied up in his estate. It was beautiful, and she had a good feeling that it would sell soon. Don was having the entire interior of the house and the guest house painted, so he had been staying with a friend. She had asked why he hadn't just moved onto the yacht. He explained that it was getting detailed and thoroughly overhauled because he had had an offer on it. When she had expressed disappointment about them no longer having such a boat, he had assured her that with the boys now part of the family, he was in the market for a bigger one that would more comfortably accommodate the four of them plus any friends who came to visit.

She loved him so. He was willing to upgrade his home and his yacht for his new family. She couldn't wait to get settled and invite friends to Miami to see her new luxurious lifestyle. *Life is falling into place,* said Beth, to herself. Here she was on her way to Miami to buy a mansion – unbelievable! Her sons were safe in the care of good friends, so worrying about coming home soon was off the table. She had felt uneasy about Jack and Cindy's offer, but when she talked it over with Don, he put her at ease by pointing out the benefits of having the kids in one place surrounded by their own stuff as opposed to being babysat some days by the Johnsons and other days by the Wards. She couldn't argue. It was true, and although she wouldn't have admitted it to anyone, she now felt unencumbered.

Instead of Don picking her up in his bright yellow Porsche like on her last visit, he had sent her a text telling her to grab a cab and have it take her to a specified address. Now, the cabbie was pulling into a hole-ridden, gravel parking lot housing a nondescript cinderblock building whose sign said "extended stay suites for rent." As she checked the address with the driver to ensure he had not made a mistake, her heart sank. She gathered her luggage, paid the cabbie, and tentatively made her way to the door, dragging her suitcase behind her while making wheels tracks in the dusty gravel.

She knew Don would not be waiting for her. His message had instructed her to go to the front desk where he had left a key. She stepped into the building and onto the kelly green, indoor outdoor carpet that covered the lobby's concrete floor. As her eyes adjusted to the dim light, she felt the same stifling humidity inside as she had felt outside the air-conditioned cab. A raised counter was on her left, and she could only assume it was the front desk. The woman behind the desk must have heard the suitcase wheels rolling on the hard floor announcing someone was coming up behind her. Ignoring the fact that it might be a guest, she chose to play a couple more moves of her online solitaire game. Finally, swiveling around to face Beth, she rose slowly from her chair and ambled over to the counter.

She was a portly woman, well over three hundred

pounds, probably in her early sixties although it was hard to tell. Her dyed red hair, with its two-inch gray roots, was piled on top of her head haphazardly, and a pencil was stuck in the side of the haystack. She wore little makeup except for thick turquoise eye shadow, false black eyelashes, and coral pink lipstick. Her clothing was four sizes too small and consisted of skin-tight, black yoga pants and a lime green tank top emphasizing her multiple abdominal rolls of blubber. The spaghetti straps of her tank top could not support her heavy bosom or her name tag, which sat at a severe angle making one cock their head if they were to read the name Buhla. Her hands were manly – the only hint of anything feminine was the chipped coral polish that had once completely covered the thick fingernails stained yellow with nicotine.

"How can I help you?" she asked Beth. The paper of her lit cigarette stuck to her bottom lip as she spoke.

"Mr. Don Lyons has left me a key," replied Beth.

"You Mrs. Lyons?"

"Yes, I am. Do you need to see some ID?" asked Beth as she began to open her purse.

"No, honey, I really don't care who you are," said the desk clerk. Just as she was about to turn around to retrieve the key, a long line of ash fell from her cigarette onto the desk. With one quick swipe with the back of her hand, Buhla pushed it onto the floor. The caliber of the accommodation was quickly sinking in, and Beth was beginning to feel queasy. She took the key from the ash-covered hand and made her way to the elevator opposite the desk. The elevator door slowly opened, almost as if the heat and humidity were hard on it, too. The trip to the third floor was agonizingly slow as Beth was forced to breathe in the elevator's stagnant air.

As the elevator door opened, the smell of stale smoke

assaulted her nose. The hallway was dimly lit but not dim enough to suit Beth. She could still see that the walls were covered with ten-year-old wallpaper that had been peeled off randomly perhaps by some bored, mischievous child. The walls were scuffed and nicked from countless pieces of luggage and careless guests. The tall, black ashtray sitting next to the elevator had been forced to hold several empty pop cans and a host of junk food litter, which was attempting an escape onto the brown carpet. The wall to wall carpeting was threadbare in front of the elevator door and down the center of the hallway from years of foot traffic.

Beth opened the door to room 308, hoping their private space would be in better shape. She was immediately disappointed by the sight and smell of their oasis. The same worn out, brown carpet covered the cement floor. The queen bed was covered with a quilted bedspread whose threads were so worn, much of the quilting pattern had dissolved. Its once bright yellow and green floral pattern, now, had the look of flowers that had faded miserably in the hot summer sun.

The small space designated as the kitchen was just that – small. It consisted of about fifteen feet of counter space interrupted by an ancient white range with black coil burners. The oven was narrow; no one would ever be able to fit a roaster into it. There was a single, aluminum sink that had lost its shine. It was dull with a short faucet whose base was heavily corroded with minerals and rust. The upper cabinets, all three of them, held old melmac dishes made of durable plastic that not even the most careless child could break. The large plates, that were supposed to be white, were now discolored with age, appearing slightly yellow with multiple slash marks made by kitchen knives. The small plates, cups, and saucers were brown, apparently meant to complement the swaying wheat motif that was faded on the dinner plates.

The lower cabinets held the cookware, which consisted of two sizes of pots with their lids, minus the knobs, and two sizes of skillets. All were made of very light aluminum, hardly a chef's choice. Next, she opened the drawers, slowly, half expecting either cockroaches, geckos, or a mouse to scamper quickly out of sight. Most of the drawers were empty, but one held an assortment of mismatched silverware. The counter top was old style Formica. It was turquoise accented with small, gold starbursts. She was sure she had seen it on reruns of *Bewitched* or *I Dream of Jeannie.* Its edging was a strip of grooved aluminum that gaped here and there due to the occasional missing screw. *Thank God, we won't have to use this kitchen,* thought Beth.

Happily moving away from the kitchen, she placed her suitcase on the bed and proceeded to unpack. Grabbing her toiletry bag, she walked into the bathroom. He heart sank once again. *Why am I surprised? It matches the rest of the place.* There was a single pedestal sink offering no place for anything, not even a toothbrush. The plug for the sink was a brittle, rubber stopper hooked to the faucet by a small beaded chain. A perpetual drip from the cold water tap had left a gray trail where the constant dripping had worn away the sink's finish.

The harvest gold bathtub was a mere five feet long but at least added some color to the room. Its porcelain finish was long gone, replaced by a dull, gray tint, that Beth prayed wasn't dirt or grime. There was a shower head, or rather a small nozzle, protruding out of the white, wall board that resembled fake tiles. At one time, it may have served its purpose, but now it was coming unglued from the wall behind it, and Beth wondered how much mold clung to its underside. She could fit under the nozzle but had no idea how Don could ever shower here. A sliding, accordion plastic door replaced the typical shower curtain. Its track was covered in goop that was no doubt a mixture of soap scum and mineral residue from the hard water, making it possible for Beth to slide it only when she used both hands. The nearby pitted aluminum bar accommodated two bath size, white towels that looked as threadbare as the carpet.

Since there was no place for her makeup bag, Beth brought it back into the bedroom/kitchen/dining room and placed it on the small, round, oak table that was supposed to be the dining table but was now going to double as her vanity. As she looked around the room, she noticed the television. It wasn't a flat screen but a large, bulky square one from the '80s. The floor to ceiling drapes matched the exhausted bedspread and framed a sliding glass door. *Well, at least we have a balcony,* she thought. As she pulled back the drapes, she saw it overlooked the parking lot, which had a variety of weeds growing out of every crack.

Why was Don staying here? Even in college, when she was watching her money on a tight budget, she had never stayed in a place that was so sad. If she weren't already motivated, this place would have certainly given her the incentive to find them a new home immediately, if not sooner! Beth finished unpacking. She had brought enough clothes for about two weeks, and her open-ended ticket would allow her to stay as long as necessary. She placed her empty suitcase against the wall near the dining table.

Normally, with little else to do, she would have ventured out for a walk around the area to stretch her legs and get her bearings. But there was no way she was going to be alone in this neighborhood, and she had no desire to go down to the desk and chat with Buhla. She wasn't tired, so a nap was of no interest. There was always the television – she prayed it worked. It did, but the remote didn't. It didn't matter; the smattering of channels carried nothing of interest anyway. The card on the bedside table said the Internet was available, for a fee, of course. She was able to connect with her iPad and immediately began thinking about the house search. While leaning against the headboard, she began looking for places for sale, but her unfamiliarity with the area they should live in made researching futile. She also knew that many large homes would not be posted online because of privacy but that a realtor specializing in selling estates would have the listings.

First, they needed a real estate agent. Then she remembered Cole. In the Keys last winter, she and Don had met him and his wife at a strip club and then had taken them back to the yacht for a night of swinging. Cole was a realtor. Although the couple did not live in Miami, surely he could recommend someone there. Beth closed her eyes trying to remember which company Cole had said he worked for.

The next thing she knew, she heard a tapping sound. Her eyes fluttered for only a second, then she fell back asleep when a louder, more forceful knock brought her back to consciousness as she realized the sound was coming from the hall. Beth groggily got to her feet and walked to the door. Looking through the peephole, her heart skipped a beat when she recognized her husband. Removing the chain, she flung open the door and threw her arms around Don's neck, causing him to take a step backward in order to regain his balance.

"Hi, sweetheart. I'm so glad you are here," said Beth,

covering his neck with kisses.

"Me, too, babe," said Don as their lips locked into a deep kiss. "Let's take this inside," he said as he nudged her toward the doorway. "I see you found the place okay."

"At first, I thought the cabbie made a mistake. Don, this place is awful. Why would you pick it?"

"Because of the location. I have business in the area almost every day, so it's convenient."

"Oh, God, I hope we aren't going to be here long."

"Me, too, baby, but I'm sure you'll find us a place soon."

"Yeah, I was just thinking about that. I guess the first step is to find a realtor. Do you remember who Cole worked for?"

"Cole who?"

"You know, Cole and Viv, from the Keys."

"I sure do remember Viv, mighty hard to forget that pretty little piece of ass," said Don with a faraway look in his eyes, as if he were recalling a great meal.

"Okay, babe. That's enough about Viv. How about Cole?"

"Cole who?" teased Don.

"Do you remember what real estate company he worked for?"

"No, not a clue."

"Then I guess I'll just look for agents who specialize in estates."

"Did you get the financial stuff all organized, so you can handle the down payment and start paying the mortgage in case my place doesn't sell for a while?"

"Yes, I have it all sorted. My portfolios have all been cashed in and transferred to my account in Kendrick."

"Then the first order of business is to get your name added to my bank account, so we can transfer those funds here."

"Yes, good idea. I want to be as organized as possible should we find a home soon. I am so excited!"

"Me, too, baby. Me, too," said Don as he ran his hands up Beth's back, taking her white tank top and bra off along the way.

"Mmm," murmured Beth. "I like the way you think." Beth clamped her eager mouth over Don's and pushed her tongue into his. His tongue explored hers while his fingers found her already erect nipples. He pinched them between his fingers, then gently pulled at them.

"Yes," whispered Beth, while Don bent his head down and sucked her nipple into his mouth, rolling his tongue over it. He moved to her other breast, repeating this move, and sucking more firmly. Beth could feel the moisture between her legs and wanted Don now.

"Fuck me. Please, just fuck me."

"Anything you want, Mrs. Lyons." They both stumbled to the bed pulling off their clothes along the way.

Not taking any chances, Beth grabbed the worn, shabby bedspread and pulled it off, letting it fall in a heap onto the worn carpet. She lay back into the bed pulling Don on top of her. She spread her legs widely and grabbed his fully erect, throbbing cock sheathing him with her wet pussy.

"Ahh, yes, that feels great, baby," grunted Don and forced his rod deeper and faster with each shove of his pelvis. Beth matched each of his thrusts, wrapping her legs around him, ankles crossed, forcing him deep inside her quivering pussy.

"God, I'm cuming already!" yelled Beth.

"Go, baby. I'm right there, too."

Don shuddered as he filled Beth with his warm cum.

"I've missed you so much, Don," said Beth, holding

Don's head between her hands and looking deeply into his eyes.

"I know, babe. But things are about to change drastically for us."

"I can't wait," said Beth, tenderly. Don silently responded with a wink.

Chapter 14

The next day when Don left for work, Beth's day was already planned. The evening before, they had found a real estate agent, and Beth had made arrangements to meet with Bernice that morning. Selling multi-million dollar estates offered immense commissions, and Bernice was very motivated to add a nice chunk of change to her bank account. Bernice was going to attempt to set up a couple of viewings for that afternoon. Beth was to see them first, narrow down the prospects to three or four choices, then Don would step in and view them as well.

Beth took a cab to Bernice's office. This was no typical office or realtor. The building was dark brown brick surrounded by impeccable professional landscaping. Beth stepped into the building and immediately felt a soothing coolness descend thanks to a high powered air conditioner that obviously worked well. The receptionist asked Beth her name and then called Bernice. In a moment, a very attractive woman in her late fifties walked toward her out of a glass-enclosed office. Bernice stood about five feet eight inches tall and was of slim build. Her pewter-colored hair was cut in an angled bob framing her face and fair skin that was without a blemish or age spot. She wore just enough makeup to accentuate her large, brown eyes, and her high cheekbones were highlighted with a light stroke of a rosy pink blush that matched her pale rose lipstick. Bernice wore a two piece, gray tweed suit with a soft pink blouse underneath. A simple short string of pearls and a matching pearl bracelet finished off her ensemble. Her black, kitten-heel pumps were perfect for someone who was on her feet most of the day.

Beth was ushered into the realtor's office and invited to take a seat. She sank back into the charcoal gray, leather barrel chair and had no sooner crossed her legs when the receptionist entered the office carrying a tray with two glasses and a pitcher of freshly made lemonade.

"Thank you, Linda," said Bernice. "Would you care for a drink?"

"That would be lovely. I'm not used to the high temperature and humidity you have here."

"I know what you mean. Even those of us born and raised here start to wilt around this time of year until late fall." Bernice filled each glass, then replaced the pitcher on the tray. Raising her glass in a toast she said, "To a successful venture in finding your family a new home." *And me a nice commission,* she said to herself.

"Amen to that," responded Beth, clinking her glass on Bernice's in response.

The next week Beth spent with Bernice viewing various properties. After spending time in one luxurious home after the other, it was torture to have to go back to the shambles she and Don were currently living in. She had taken a cab everywhere, not allowing Bernice to pick her up or drop her off out of embarrassment.

She had called the boys twice every day, and everything with them seemed to be going well. With each call, she gave them an update on the houses she was seeing. After viewing fourteen prospects, Bernice admitted they had exhausted all the current listings. Now, she suggested Beth narrow it down to three based on those that best matched her wish list. Beth sat down with Don one evening and went over all she had seen. She then called Bernice to set up appointments for the three of them to go back and show Don her favorites.

Beth and Don walked to Don's loaner car, a 2006 Impala. The first time she had seen it, she was stunned, demanding to know where his eye-popping yellow Porsche was. Don had explained that his lease had been up several weeks before and he didn't want to lease or buy another vehicle without her input, knowing they would need something more family-friendly. The loaner was a spare car that one of Don's friends had. He offered Don the use of it without charge, and Don had taken him up on it. Beth had been embarrassed for Bernice to see their vehicle and had quickly explained the scenario. Bernice said it sounded like a savvy, money-saving, plan and assured Beth they could take her Mercedes to all appointments.

After they had toured the homes, Don came away equally as impressed as his wife. Bernice drove them back to her office and encouraged them not to wait too long to make a decision. On the way back to the motel, Don recommended they relax a little. He could take some time off the next day and suggested they mull over selecting their new home while out enjoying one of Miami's beautiful golf courses. Beth had golfed a few times and had enjoyed it enough to know she would like to try it again.

It was a beautiful, hot, sunny, late afternoon in Miami. Beth was looking forward to golfing with Don. She and

Richard had always talked about taking golf lessons when the boys were older – something for them to enjoy throughout their retirement together. Tears stung her eyes as her thoughts wandered briefly to Richard. Poor Richard... too many years were stolen from her and her sons. Her marriage to him and their family unit felt like a lifetime ago.

But she was starting a new and exciting chapter in her life, which brought her back to the moment. Don had decided their loaner car was an inappropriate choice to drive to the prestigious club, so they called a cab instead. As they drove to the Riviera Country Club in Coral Gables, on the west side of Ormond Beach, she couldn't imagine what it would be like to be a member of such an exclusive club, but she was sure she would adjust! Beth hoped her pink skirt and collared, sleeveless top-sans bra would be acceptable. Don certainly seemed to approve as he eyed her nipples before running his thumb across them before they got into the car.

The scenic drive went by quickly, and they were soon passing through the grand entrance of antique, cement columns positioned on either side of the road. The cabbie slowed, then stopped in front of the hacienda style clubhouse at the valet stand. As Beth's door was opened by one valet, Don exited the opposite side.

"This is so exciting, Don!" exclaimed Beth.

"I already called ahead, and they have my clubs in the cart. We need to grab you a set. I'll let them know – you wait here," said Don as he headed toward the pro shop.

Don reappeared minutes later and walked Beth to their cart. They watched as the attendee placed Beth's rental clubs in the back beside Don's bag.

"There are no scheduled tee times here. First come, first serve. This time of day, because of the heat, it won't be busy at all. In fact, we may have the course all to our-selves," explained Don. "We are only going to play nine holes today. I want you to take it easy! But let's pick up a couple of drinks first."

Don ordered four vodka and tonics and gave a membership number. With their drinks in hand, they jumped into the golf cart and headed to the first hole.

Don grabbed the drivers from both bags. He handed Beth's driver to her and positioned to tee off.

"I will help you swing by swing today, as well as discuss strategies regarding the slope, headwinds, et cetera."

Beth said, "Wait a minute. We haven't discussed our rules of play yet."

"What do you mean? I thought you did a little research and understood the fundamentals of the game," said Don, slightly annoyed.

"Oh, I did, but I thought it would be more fun to play by our own rules," smiled Beth.

"Hmm. What you have in mind?" grinned Don.

"If I swing and hit the ball off the tee, you have to kiss me," said Beth.

"What if you don't?"

"Then you get whatever you want from me."

"I see. And what, pray tell, are the rest of the rules?" Don asked as he leaned on his driver.

"Okay. If I hit the ball into play at all – you have to finger me or suck my nipples."

"And what if you don't?" chuckled Don.

"Your putter gets stroked, of course!"

"I like these rules," laughed Don.

"If either of us hits the ball into the trees, we fuck there," said Beth seriously.

"What if I get a birdie or par?" asked Don. "Before you

answer, you should know that I'm a decent golfer."

"I blow you, Mr. Smart Ass."

"What if I drain the hole?" teased Don.

"What's that?" Beth asked quizzically.

"It means I sink the ball into the cup," explained Don.

"Oh," said Beth, "I will give you a very special target to aim for to make that happen."

Don replied, "And on number four, I want you on all fours, to receive my shaft."

"I think I'm going to like this game very much," laughed Beth. "And you are right – it looks like we are completely alone out here today!"

With their new rules established, Don teed off and smacked the ball down the fairway. He then helped Beth into position at the ladies' tee and directed her through her swing.

"This is much harder than it looks," said Beth.

"Keep trying. Square your shoulders, head down, hips rotating through the ball," said Don patiently.

Beth attempted to strike the ball but only succeeded in whiffing it.

"Uh-oh," said Don." I think you owe me something now."

"Name it," Beth said proudly.

"Let's drop out at my ball, and you give me a hand job on the way there."

"Deal," laughed Beth as she climbed into the golf cart. Don unzipped his shorts before he climbed in beside Beth. She took a sip of her drink, rolling the melting ice cubes over her tongue.

"Sorry, I just can't resist," said Beth as she bent her head for her cold tongue to meet her hand around Don's already stiff cock.

She ran her tongue up and down, then swirled around

the head, before removing her mouth. She pumped up and down with her left hand tightly while thumbing the underside of the tip of his cock.

"God, I'm going to cum already. Get ready to swallow it, baby," ordered Don.

Beth obediently bent her head down again and, opening her mouth, took Don's hard dick in her mouth just as he exploded his spluge toward the back of her throat. She swallowed every drop, sat upright, and took a swig of her drink.

"Thanks for the protein shake," giggled Beth.

"Anytime, honey, anytime!" Don chuckled. He stopped the cart at his ball and zipped up his golf shorts. "Let's play some more!"

Beth successfully hit her ball down the fairway close to Don's. "Lucky shot," he half muttered under his breath.

He smiled and walked over to Beth. Kissing her deeply, he slid his right hand under her skirt to find that she was wearing crotchless panties. Beth chuckled at the surprised look on Don's face. He easily found the opening in the lacy fabric and shoved two fingers up into Beth's pussy.

"Yes," breathed Beth.

"You like this?" asked Don and he pumped in and out of her.

Beth couldn't answer but leaned into Don as he finger-fucked her and simultaneously rubbed her clit with his thumb.

"Don, I'm going to cum," said Beth.

Don felt her pussy walls clamp down around his fingers as he continued to push inside. When Beth stilled, he removed his hand from under Beth's golf skirt and, grabbing her shoulders, probed her mouth with his tongue.

"I think this heat and sun have made us very horny, Beth. Are you sure we shouldn't head back?"

"No, I want to try hitting the ball some more!" Beth said with a pout.

"Okay, okay. But at this rate, we aren't making much progress," laughed Don.

"Well, I will take one shot for every two or three of yours, then," said Beth.

Don agreed and took his next three shots without incident. He parred the hole in five, then showed Beth how to putt, which came rather naturally to her.

"It's just like goofy golf!" exclaimed Beth.

"Not even close, darling. Time to blow me."

Beth dropped to her knees and unzipped Don's shorts. She took his semi-stiff cock into her mouth and swirled her tongue around it as Don grasped the back of her head, pulling her down the length of him. He wrapped his fingers through her long, red hair and pushed and pulled while Beth's mouth, tongue, and lips pumped him like a piston. Up and down, she slid her mouth over the heat of Don's throbbing cock.

"Damn it, I'm going to cum again already!" exclaimed Don.

Forcing her head into his crotch, he held her there until he exploded once more into her hungry mouth and throat.

Beth zipped Don up before standing up and trying to wipe the grass stains from her knees.

The tee for the second hole was challenging with the stand of trees on either side. Both Beth and Don shanked their balls into the woods. Understanding their new set of golf rules, they wordlessly went into the woods to retrieve their balls. Don pushed Beth against a large oak tree yanking her white blouse up to her chin while loosening his shorts and letting them drop around his ankles. He clamped his eager mouth around her nipple and began to suck, while the thumb of his right hand was working the other nipple, causing a heat wave to travel down toward Beth's sopping, wet pussy. She grabbed Don's face pulling him from her nipple and, while kissing him, she probed his mouth with her slippery and eager tongue. Don yanked her skirt down and pushed her back and buttocks up the tree as he stuffed his cock inside her pussy. Beth reached up to the branch slightly above her head to grab on to for support. She wrapped her legs around Don's hips and hoisted herself up and down to meet Don's lustful thrusts. Feeling the soft skin of her ass and lower back being ravaged by the tree bark only intensified the orgasm welling up inside her. She felt herself cum as Don shot his hot load deep within her.

After two minutes of panting against one another, all they could do was look at each other and laugh.

"Let me help you down from there," said Don as he easily lifted Beth, twirled her around, and set her back down on her feet.

"You're going to be sore tomorrow."

"Tomorrow? I'm already feeling it. Am I bleeding?" asked Beth as she turned to show Don her rear.

"Wow, babe. You give a new meaning to bark burn!" he laughed.

"Very funny. I've never even experienced rug burn, but now this!"

"I'll give you some TLC as soon as we get back," assured Don. "I am looking forward to the fourth hole now!"

True to his word, after Don sunk his ball on the fourth

hole, he positioned Beth on all fours in the middle of the putting green. Pushing her skirt up, he aimed his cock between the lacy slit of her panties once again and pushed his full length and girth into her. Beth braced herself and took all of him with every forceful thrust. He drove into her like a rutting deer, and Beth received like a bitch in heat. The hot sun, mixed with alcohol, was quite an aphrodisiac –that, plus the time and distance of separation for the newlyweds.

"Fuck me hard," demanded Beth.

Don responded back with his cock, almost knocking Beth off her already tender knees.

Beth loved the feel and sound of his balls slapping her thighs, although she was still feeling sore from the tree. She had started to lose count as to how many times they fucked or how many orgasms they each had. *Life with Don was going to be a fairy-tale,* she thought. *There is nothing I will deny him.*

Don continued his rear-entry pussy assault while thumbing Beth's sensitive clit. She came only seconds before he did. Don half-collapsed on Beth and looked around to make sure they were still alone on the course.

"Oh, my God," was all Don could say.

"I knew I was going to be sore from exercising and walking today, but honestly I had no idea how sore," said Beth as she rolled over in a fit of laughter.

Don caught her laughing jag, and rolling on top of her, kissed her passionately and languidly.

"I love you, Don," said Beth.

"Let's go back and finish this honeymoon more comfortably," responded Don.

Between blowjobs in the bushes and groping on the greens, the amateur golfers managed to come to a decision about which estate to purchase. Beth was giddy with excitement. The property they chose satisfied her entire wish list. The house was amazing and the grounds breathtaking with an in-ground swimming pool, lazy river, and a dock for the new yacht they would buy next. Her head was already swimming with color palettes and design decisions. The price tag was just over two million, but they hoped Bernice could negotiate several hundred thousand off the asking price.

To celebrate, they ended up at a diner for burgers and shakes before heading back to the motel. While waiting for their food, Beth checked her phone and discovered her realtor back home had left a message. Although it was past business hours, Beth took a chance and gave her a call. As if the day hadn't been exciting enough, Beth learned someone had placed an offer on her house slightly below the asking price. Full of smiles, she ended the call, and gave Don the news. They decided not to counter and accept what the buyer had offered. What a day it had been, one of the best of her life! She couldn't wait to call the kids and share all her news!

Beth needed to go back to Ohio and take care of several things, including the packing up of her house. She had decided to offer the new owners the opportunity to buy, from her, all the furniture and some of the other things she wouldn't need in Florida. She and Don would be buying all new furniture and wouldn't have the need for a lawn mower and various other things. She also needed to be around to take care of the paperwork that went with selling her home.

Now that she had a bank account in Florida, she could have the funds transferred to the bank there. She would be able to offer a hefty down payment on the new estate and comfortably make the mortgage payments. Once Don's estate sold, the money from the sale would be invested and replace her portfolio. Don suggested that he accompany her to Kendrick to help pack up her house, and she immediately took him up on his offer.

Several days later, Don and Beth stepped off the plane in Kendrick into the arms of the boys, who were with Cindy at the airport to pick them up The boys were excited to see her and had all kinds of questions about their new swimming pool and bedrooms. It warmed her heart to finally see them excited about the move. Although she was home, the boys would continue to stay with Jack and Cindy while the Anderson house was dismantled. While Beth took care of the financial paperwork with the realtor and her banker, Don remained a trooper, packing, and labeling box after box, knowing it would all be worth it in the end. The new family had agreed to purchase much of Beth's furniture; almost everything else had been boxed up when Don received an urgent phone call from work forcing him to get back on a plane and prematurely head back to Miami. It would take another few days for Beth to tie up all the loose ends before she could make her way back to Florida to hopefully co-sign the deed to their new house.

Chapter 15

eth had spent a number of days in Kendrick taking care of business and spending time with her kids and friends. She knew there wouldn't likely be many trips back to Ohio, and as she stood in her driveway for the last time, she began to reminisce. She could remember when she and Richard bought the house; they were so young, just beginning their lives together. She could remember holding Max in her arms while sitting on the front step watching Richard cut the grass. She remembered how long it took the two of them to assemble the kids' swing set, finally having to call a neighbor over to help. She remembered the block parties they had been part of and taking the boys Halloweening, year after year, in their neighborhood. These were wonderful memories associated with the house. She had been so excited about the move, she had almost forgotten to remember. Now that they would live in the heart of one of America's playgrounds and have plenty of room to entertain, she was sure her friends would be flying south, giving her little need to return to Kendrick.

After she and Don had eloped, she had called her parents and informed them of her marriage and her eventual move to Florida. Although they would still be a three-hour drive apart, she wanted to work on mending their estranged relationship, so her sons would have grandparents in their lives. She had grown apart from her parents. Her dad had been a very busy cardiac surgeon, always too busy saving lives to find time for his daughters. Her mom had not contributed to society much, except for helping the economy by paying the large booze bill she rung up each year at the country club. Yes, this move to Florida was the right thing to do for so many reasons.

Beth had stopped at Jack and Cindy's on her way to the airport. With their personal belongings in a truck on its way to Florida, the only thing Beth still had to deal with was her mini-van. It was seven years old and not worth a great deal. For the time being, it would be parked at Jack and Cindy's until she could catch her breath, advertise, and sell it. Saying goodbye to the kids was difficult, but she left them with the promise that she would let them pick out their own bedrooms and beds once the purchase of the estate was final. The Wards had offered to accompany the kids to Florida when Beth and Don were settled in their new home. They wanted to be sure the boys would arrive safely, and they were excited to see the Lyons's estate.

While waiting for her flight to board, Beth texted Don telling him everything was taken care of at her end and she would see him later that day. She hadn't heard from Bernice lately but figured she and Don had been communicating in her absence. Beth was looking forward to being back with her husband and finding out the status of their real estate offer. By the time she boarded the plane, she still hadn't gotten a response from Don. *What's new?* she asked herself. As she sat on the plane, she opened one of the half a dozen interior design magazines she had purchased. As she went through them page by page, she made notes regarding ideas for each room. Beth loved interior design, and to have a whole house to decorate, and the money to do it with, was a dream come true.

Between flights, Beth checked her phone. Still no messages from Don. He knew she was flying back today, so he may not have been watching for any communication from her. Oh well, she would see him in a couple of hours. She was so ready for a slow, comfortable screw – the drink kind and the sex kind!

The plane touched down on schedule, and Beth made her way to the baggage claim. After retrieving her bag from the carousel, she searched the crowd for Don. She hadn't expected him to pick her up, but due to their lack of communication, she wasn't sure. He was nowhere to be found, so she jumped into a cab, heading back to the dismal hotel. The driver pulled into the pothole-filled, gravel parking lot, and Beth paid the fare. The place didn't look any better than before she left, but she didn't care anymore. Soon she would never again have to worry about a dump like this. Beth let herself into the lobby giving a nod to Buhla, who looked as ravishing as ever. Buhla laid Beth's key on the counter, and with a quick thanks, Beth walked over to the elevator. Getting off the elevator, she opened room 308. She supposed she needed to unpack, not knowing the status of the estate purchase. Her heart skipped a beat when she opened the closet and saw that all of Don's clothes were gone! *Our offer must have been accepted, and he has already moved some of his stuff out of the motel.* She couldn't wait to follow suit!

Once again, she tried to call him but ended up with a recording telling her the call could not be completed as dialed. *Well,* she said to herself, *Bernice will know what's going on.* She gave the realtor a call, knowing there would be much to finalize with many papers to be filled out and required signatures.

"This is Bernice. How can I help you?"

"Hi, Bernice, this is Beth Lyons. I just flew back from Ohio, and I was wondering the status of the estate we were interested in."

"Hi, Beth, well, now I'm a little confused. Just this afternoon, your husband called me and said there was a change in plans, and you were no longer interested in buying a new home."

"What!" exclaimed Beth "That's ridiculous. We've never discussed anything like that."

"Well, I don't know what to tell you. I guess you two need to talk. Please let me know if you still need my services."

"Thanks, Bernice. We'll be in touch."

Bernice wasn't the only one who was confused. Beth simply could not wrap her head around what she had just learned. She began to get a sick feeling in the pit of her stomach –a feeling of dread, of doom.

Over the next hour, she paced and re-dialed Don numerous times. Each call ended with the same recorded message. Now, in a near panic, she tried to calm herself down. Sitting in the room by herself was not helping. Maybe the workers at his estate would know how to get in touch with him. Calling a taxi, she arrived at the familiar mansion and walked up to the front door. Nothing had changed at the estate since her last visit. The modern designed home still looked exquisite with its abundance of large windows allowing one to see clear through the house to the magnificent in-ground pool in the back. The grounds were still full of beautiful blooms, and the fountain opposite the front door still trickled its soothing sound. But something wasn't right. Don's yellow Porsche sat parked in the circular drive; he had said the lease was up. As she approached the front door, it was opened by an older woman in a maid's uniform.

"Is Mr. Lyons here?"

"I have not seen him today, but if you go around back to the guest house, he may be there." Just as the maid was about to close the door, a well-dressed man who looked to be in his late sixties appeared.

"Can I help you?" he asked.

"Yes, perhaps. I'm looking for my husband, Don Lyons. Is he home?"

"Unfortunately, I haven't seen him since the day before yesterday. As you can see, the grass needs to be cut, and the pool needs attending to. I have a good mind to let him go."

"You mean like fire him?"

"Yes. He is no good to me if he doesn't show up for work."

"Wait a minute. I don't know what's going on here. Doesn't Don own this estate, the Porsche, and the yacht?"

"Madame, you are the one married to the man – you must know the answer to your questions."

"But that is what he has told me. I've stayed here with Don, we have driven the car many times, and we went down to the Keys together on the yacht."

"Really? That's interesting, because I own the estate, the car, and the yacht. Don is my caretaker and lives in back in the guest house. I'm afraid he has been less than honest with you."

Reality began to sink in, and Beth turned very pale. Her breathing changed, and it was clear she was hyperventilating. She leaned heavily on the door frame, steadying herself with her hands.

"Are you all right?" asked the gentleman.

"No, I feel very light-headed. I'm afraid I might pass out."

"Come in and sit down until you feel better," he said as he guided her to the expensive white chaise she had sat on before- under very different circumstances.

"Hannah," said the man, as he summoned his maid. "Please go out to the guest house and see if Don is there."

"Yes, sir," she replied as she headed toward the back door.

"I don't know what to tell you. By the way, my name is Wayne."

"I'm Beth," she said as she looked up at him sheepishly. She was pretty sure what Hannah would find. It was sinking in that she had been duped. Then she remembered her money.

"Oh, God. Oh, God," she said as terror rose inside her, and she began to cry. "I cashed in all my financial portfolio and the money from the recent sale of my house in Ohio and put it all in our joint bank account here. He said he was selling this place, so we could buy a bigger home – we recently married, and I have two little boys." The thought of her kids made her break down completely and she began to sob into her hands, covering her face.

Beth knew she had to call the bank immediately, yet she wanted to put it off as long as possible. If her worst fears came true, if her money was all gone, she would have no choice but to face the cold, hard truth; then she would have reason to panic. Right now, a tiny sliver of hope remained. Her hands were shaking so badly, she could not dial the bank's number. Wayne dialed it for her and handed her the phone. In a quivering voice, she gave the teller her account number and security code. Beth could hear the teller making keystrokes. Her hands were shaking and moist, her heart was thumping, and her throat felt tight. Finally, after what seemed like forever, he gave her the news, "Your balance, Mrs. Lyons, is one hundred dollars."

"Can you tell me when the money was withdrawn?"

"Several hundreds of thousands of dollars were withdrawn over the last four days with each of eight transactions. A total of two point seven million dollars has been removed from your joint account."

To add insult to injury, Hannah reappeared confirming what Beth already knew. Don's guest house had been cleaned out. Beth felt compelled to do something, to find the lying, cheating fucker, and get her money back. Her shock was slowly turning to rage.

"I need to call the police now."

"Well, of course, that's your choice, but from what you've told me, Don hasn't done anything illegal. You said the money was in a joint account, so he had the legal right to withdraw it without your permission. It's as dirty and unethical as you can get but not illegal."

"Oh, God, what do I do now?"

"You can call the police, explain the situation, and if you know what he's driving, they may agree to try to find him for you, but I doubt they can charge him with anything."

Beth did call the Miami police and explained her situation. And just like Wayne had predicted, they told her they would tell their patrolmen to keep an eye out for the car, but they would not assign any officers to the case – as a case didn't exist. What they couldn't tell Beth was that they had been watching Don Lyons for months as part of a sting operation in conjunction with the FBI. With Beth's information, they would now put more effort into finding him, effort that they were not able to admit to her.

Although the police were not much help, Beth felt better after sharing her story with the authorities. She had several hundred dollars in her wallet, the hundred he had so generously left her in their bank account, her personal belongings which were on their way to Miami and her mini-van. That was it! Not only was she broke, but she was also brokenhearted and unbelievably embarrassed. Tom and her friends had had their reservations, but she had known better. Despite having to face her friends, she needed to get back to Kendrick where she felt safe. *Oh, God, where will I live? One thing at a time,* she told herself as the anxiety began to rise within her again. *I need to get back to Kendrick and clear my head, so I can make some decisions.*

Her next call was to Jack and Cindy. She was only able to talk to their voicemail and simply said she needed to fly home and would be home later that evening. She told them she would text her flight information and asked them to pick her up at the airport. Cindy received the email and immediately assumed there had been a snafu with the selling of Beth's home and that she needed to be present to take care of the problem.

Wayne was kind enough to drive her back to the seedy hotel in the bright yellow Porsche that Beth had fallen in love with. The sight of it sickened her now; it was a reminder of the depth of Don's deceit. She started to tear up again. She was in shock about the present and scared to death about the future. She thanked Wayne profusely for the ride, and as she walked back into the dump, she prayed that Don had come to his senses and he would be waiting for her upstairs. In her heart, she knew better, but grief had a way of bypassing common sense.

The run-down accommodation was the same as she had left it. Now it was clear why they had been staying in a one-star hotel. She quickly threw her belongings into her suitcase. She couldn't wait to get the hell out of there and put this piece of the nightmare behind her. She paused at the front desk to hand Buhla the key. Noticing Beth's luggage, Buhla stopped her, "You checking out, honey?"

"Yes."

"Well, there is a little matter of a not-so-little bill that somebody needs to pay." Beth's throat began to tighten again at this latest financial assault. Buhla ignored Beth's emotional response, simply pushing the bill worth almost twelve hundred dollars toward her, while Beth handed over her credit card. As the transaction finished, the cab she had ordered pulled up to the door. Thank God, she was on her way to the airport, away from Don's world of lies and deceit.

Beth had multiple hours while flying home to finally put all the pieces together. Now so many things made sense. The difficulty she always seemed to have contacting Don was not because he was working so hard; now she knew her constant calls and texts must have been just a pain in his ass. He hadn't bothered to talk to her because he had no feelings for her. He hadn't cared about her sons because he had no reason to. He knew he would never need to have a relationship with them. The thought of her innocent and trusting kids being part of Don's scheme made her sick to her stomach.

No wonder he said they couldn't stay at the estate while looking for a new house. It wasn't getting a make-over. It didn't belong to him. Wayne had explained to Beth that he lived most of the year in Europe, and it was obvious that it was when Wayne was in Monte Carlo that Don had wined and dined her at the estate and on the yacht. The reason the staff and the valet knew Don at the fancy restaurant in Miami Beach was because he had dropped Wayne and his dates off at the restaurant many times. Don often acted as a chauffeur and personal assistant to Wayne as well as the gardener and pool guy. No wonder when they had had Internet sex, Don had not been in the master suite but in the guest house – it's where he lived!

She had been so gullible. She had paid for things that she shouldn't have. She had paid for Don's wedding suit. She had paid for their very expensive wedding dinner in Vegas. Don had always paid just enough of the bills so she wouldn't become suspicious. Obviously, he wasn't the one with the Riviera Golf Club membership either. He was so damn clever. She was even ready to buy a mansion for them because his money was tied up in the estate. Now, she knew it was all lies. She couldn't begin to wrap her head around it all. Her DNA makeup couldn't begin to let her justify any part of his scam. She couldn't imagine scheming and hurting people, not just people but families, and others who had made him feel so welcome.

She had learned a very valuable lesson, and for the rest of her life, she would not forget it. No one would ever be able to hide important things from her, lie, or cheat and get away with it again.

Beth could tell the plane was beginning to descend. They would be landing within the next thirty minutes. She dried her eyes, blew her nose, and pulled herself together. Soon she would be among friends. Good friends who would not say, "I told you so"; friends who would love her and help her. Thankfully, she was nearly home.

Chapter 16

It was very late when Beth's plane finally landed in Kendrick. Cindy had put the boys to bed hours before, and Jack had followed suit some time ago leaving Cindy to make the drive to the airport. She knew she had to be the one to get her friend. Something was up. Even though Cindy had no idea what the problem was, she knew Beth would need to vent.

Beth claimed her luggage and turned around to see Cindy standing several yards back. She rushed into her friend's arms, dropping both pieces of luggage. It wasn't until then that Beth truly let her guard down and felt just how physically and emotionally exhausted she was. She immediately began to sob and was crying so hard she couldn't have relayed her story even if she had wanted to. Fellow passengers were giving the two women nothing more than a fleeting glance presuming it was a tender reunion with tears of joy. Cindy hugged her friend tightly, standing motionless until Beth's choking sobs relaxed a little into a river of quiet tears.

"Let's get out of here, honey," said Cindy, guiding her friend toward the door. "The car is nearby. We can talk there." Approaching the car, Cindy remotely popped open the trunk and unlocked the car's doors. Beth's suitcases were thrown into the trunk then both women sat in the dark, silent vehicle. Beth continued to sniff and dab her eyes with a tissue while Cindy settled herself behind the steering wheel and turned to face her friend.

"What happened?" was all Cindy needed to say for Beth to open the floodgate of tears, once again. Soon, she regained enough composure to relay the incredible nightmare she had just lived through in the past day. Beth carried on and on, seemingly getting some relief from spewing out all the details. Once she got talking, her blubbering turned to anger, and she continued ranting, not giving Cindy a chance to say anything, which was good because Cindy was absolutely speechless. Sure, she and Jack had some reservations about Don, but they had decided it was because they hadn't had much of a chance to get to know him. In the end, they had been happy for Beth and her boys. Beth concluded by admitting she had no money, no home, no husband and no job.

"Can I stay with you, Jack, and the boys until I figure this whole thing out?"

"Of course. You and the boys can stay with us as long as you need to."

"Thank you so much." That, in itself, was a relief knowing she and her sons would have a roof over their heads and food in their bellies.

They pulled into the Ward's driveway and then made their way into the house, tiptoeing down the dark hallway. Beth peeked in on Max and Matt, who were sleeping the innocent sleep of children. Beth found her way to the other guest room and crawled into bed. Surprisingly, she slept soundly, completely exhausted.

Beth awoke to any empty house. Fortunately, the Wards had continued on with their daily routine despite her. They had taken the boys to school and had both gone to work as usual. She found a note on the kitchen table from Cindy telling her to make herself at home and that they would get the boys from school. She also promised she wouldn't say anything to anyone about what had happened. Beth was relieved to read that. She was so embarrassed by her poor judgment with Don that she wanted to hide. She turned on the television and sat mindlessly staring at the screen. She thought back to how hopeless she had felt while still in Miami and how much better she had felt after telling Cindy the long, sad story.

Mustering up inner strength, she picked up her cell phone, first checking for a call from the Miami police – but there was nothing – then calling Jess. She had just shared the gist of the story before dissolving in tears again. Jess offered to come and keep her company, and Beth jumped at the offer. She didn't want to be alone, and she needed guidance as to where to start to get her life back.

Jess had dropped what she was doing to be with her friend. She knew once she got to the Wards' home, she would hear all the details. She was heartsick for Beth, and while driving over she tried to think how she and Eric could help. Beth was literally standing at the door when Jess pulled into the driveway. The reunion was full of tears and tissues. Once Beth relayed the information including all the details she could muster, she blew her nose, wiped away the tears, and asked Jess what she should do first. Jess encouraged her to be open with those folks who could possibly help her.

Tom came to mind immediately, but her pride said no. He had warned her over and over about Don, and she had told him to mind his own business. No, Tom was not a priority. Unwilling to take money from others, her first need was to find a job. She couldn't go back to work as a nurse practitioner, having been away from the profession long enough to have her licenses expire. Renewing them would take too long. No, she needed work now. Then Keely came to mind. She, Larry and Lori owned a large business. Maybe they needed some help in the bakery or catering departments especially since Larry would have to cut back some of his hours to regain his good health.

Jess sat quietly as Beth made the difficult call to Keely. Hearing Beth's story made Keely's stomach turn and Jess feel sorry for her friend all over again. She couldn't believe Don had turned out to be a criminal. Yes, she would consult with her business partners but was sure they could give Beth a job and she could stay with her for the time being, too. Beth began to cry at the generosity of the people who had been strangers less than a year ago. She expressed her thanks over and over, and by the time she hung up from the New York call, she was feeling as though she had just received some direction. She relayed the job opportunity to Jess.

Now, Beth's only concern was for her kids. Jess said not to worry. If Jack and Cindy could not continue to look after them for an extended period of time, she and Eric would. Beth hugged Jess tightly, took a deep breath, and began to make a list of the other issues she needed to attend to.

Jess had left by the time Cindy brought the kids home from school. The boys had no idea that their mom was back from Florida and were surprised and excited to see her. Immediately, they asked if she had come to get them to take them back to Florida with her, and it broke her heart to tell them they would not be moving. They seemed confused at first and then shrugged, seemingly taking it in stride.

"Does this mean we won't be changing schools?" asked Matt.

"That's right, sweetheart, you can keep going to school here."

"Yes!" said Matt, enthusiastically to the surprise of his mother.

"But it means Ben won't be coming to see us," pointed out Matt, beginning to pout.

"I know, but it means we won't be moving away from Ben, you dummy!" said big brother Max.

"Hey, Max, there is no need to call anyone names," reminded Beth.

"Oh, yeah! That's right," replied Matt. "We can still play with Ben every day."

Well, that went over just fine, thought Beth. Now, she needed to talk to the Wards about continuing to keep the boys until she got herself settled in New York City.

Once the boys were in bed, Beth relayed the conversation she had had with Keely. She expressed her gratefulness for a job and her inability to take the boys with her until she could afford her own place. Jack reminded her that they already had some custodial rights and would be happy to have them stay as long as necessary. This was a huge commitment from the Wards and brought Beth to another round of tears, this time, of relief. Beth knew she couldn't afford to sit around Kendrick. She hadn't given up hope that Don would be found in the future, but right now she had a job waiting, and so many pieces of her life hinged on making an income. She could not waste time and the next day purchased a bus ticket to the Big Apple. Jack had tried to loan her plane fare, but Beth would not hear of it. She was broke and needed to live accordingly – starting now.

Chapter 17

Happily, the bus fare was not expensive, but the number of hours sitting on the bus was arduous. Beth tried to relax during the monotonous trip, but sleep came in fits and starts. Her inability to rest was due, in part, to the less than comfortable seat but more so because of Beth's shredded emotional state.

New York City had held such happy memories, and she was afraid going back would add salt to the huge wound that would take a long time to heal. Keely, Larry, and Lori were all at the bus station when she stepped off the bottom step, bleary-eyed to say the least. Their show of love and solidarity was unexpected but so appreciated. Seeing her friend Larry looking so well after his heart attack was another reason to feel grateful. They all gathered at Keely's apartment to welcome her and discuss the job. They decided that the next day, Keely would take her to the bakery where they would fill out the appropriate forms and paperwork; if she felt ready, she could begin work the day after that. Beth would be part of the catering staff, working in the kitchen to prepare the food and also serving at catering functions. Her wage would be nowhere near that of a nurse practitioner, but it was more generous than she had expected.

The Golden Grain Patisserie was a buzz of activity. It was wedding season, and the catering side of the business was booked solid for months. She would certainly earn her paycheck, which was fine by Beth. She welcomed the diversion of hard work. Beth hadn't worked since Richard's death, and the first few weeks on the job kicked her butt. She was physically exhausted at the end of every long day but thankful for every minute of it. Because of her long hours, she had no time to think about Don or feel sorry for herself. Each day, she woke up grateful to be able to earn a living again.

The catering jobs, so far, had been mainly wedding receptions and business-related luncheons or dinners. Every client was upscale. She had never seen such opulent affairs. The Golden Grain Patisserie used nothing but the finest ingredients, their service was impeccable, and their prices high. They fed New York's wealthy and well-known, making each event eye-opening. Beth learned to make deviled eggs topped with caviar, crudités using fresh salmon flown in daily from Alaska, and sumptuous lobster mac and cheese. Expensive truffles, European cheeses, and the finest of Kobe beef were prepared for many events. Serving was not difficult work, and Beth didn't even mind the black pants, white tuxedo shirt, and black bow tie that made up her uniform.

After the first event, however, she was quick to trade in her black stilettos for a pair of more sensible shoes. She had proven to be a quick study and was great with people. Keely, Lori, and Larry were already pleased with Beth as the newest addition to their staff.

Before leaving work, Beth had checked the next day's schedule and found it intriguing. They were catering dinner to a group in Manhattan and the note on the calendar called it "naked dinner." She would ask for clarification when she went to work the following day. After returning home, she had given Max and Matt a call and was assured all was well with the kids. She and Keely had each had a glass of wine with dinner, showered, and then headed to bed. Tomorrow would be another day.

It didn't take Beth long, once she arrived at work, to find out what the day's catering gig was all about. Apparently, a group of New Yorkers met monthly for a naked dinner. The event was held in a rented venue and often catered by the Golden Grain. Some of the diners were nudists, but most were not. Some had belonged to the unique group for years while others had recently learned about it and wanted to give it a try. Every one of any age, creed, color and religion was welcome. The only thing necessary was payment for the meal and an appetite.

The premise was that without clothes there was one less barrier between people. Nudity encouraged honesty and expression of the true self. Most of the diners admitted that by the time the meal was served, they had all but forgotten they didn't have any clothes on. The big question was, did the servers need to be naked also? The answer was no. The catering staff treated the unique dinner like any other catering job.

The venue was a small hall, cozy but definitely big enough to comfortably hold the expected thirty to thirty-five guests. Beth and her crew got busy carrying dishes, linens, and food from the catering van. It was early summer, so the tablecloths boasted brightly colored gerbera daisies, and the cloth napkins were a vibrant lime green. The round tables each held five diners, and they set up eight, just to be sure. Mimicking the table cloths, fresh gerbera daisies were set in stubby, square, clear glass vases. Along with the silverware and stemware, each place setting held a white, soft square plate.

As the guests began to arrive, where coats would have

been taken off and hung up, the dinner guests removed all their clothes, leaving on only their shoes. At first, it seemed odd, even for Beth, who, as a swinger had seen plenty of flesh. But after a while, she stopped seeing the nakedness and focused on the people. From the bits of conversation she picked up, it seemed many were artsy. There were artists, a director, a Broadway dancer, a couple of understudies, a greeting card writer and a choreographer. The rest of the crowd was made up of business types and other professionals. Beth's swinger instincts kicked off and on during the event. There were some well-hung men and also some women with very perky nipples sitting atop round, firm breasts. Some lovely shaped butts on both sexes rounded out the eye-candy. It was completely expected that none of them would be swingers, so Beth kept her fantasies to herself.

The event had been short for a change, and Beth was home around eight. Keely sat in her pajamas watching a reality show, grumbling under her breath about how absurd the whole thing was.

"Hey, girlfriend," said Keely as the apartment door opened.

"Hey, yourself."

"How did the naked dinner go?"

"Great. Nice, polite people, no issues."

"I thought you'd be home relatively early, so I saved drinking a glass of wine until you got home. Would you like some?"

"I'd love some. Seeing all those nudes tonight made me wonder if you wanted to go to Quench later this week."

"Why not? I don't think there is anything scheduled for Thursday night – let's make it a date!"

"You're on!" replied Beth, giving her friend a high-five.

Chapter 18

Any reservations that Beth had about going to Quench were Don related. The last time she had been there, she felt on top of the world. Now, she was building a new life, but it would take a while for her to get over his deceit. Everywhere she turned, there was a reminder of him. He had taken enough from her; she wouldn't let him take her future, too. Just like when Richard died, the first time for everything without him had brought back painful memories. It wasn't so different this time. She realized she was grieving, once again. Grieving for the man she thought Don was; grieving for the life she thought she and her sons would be living, and grieving for her once uncomplicated life. She also knew grief was a process and couldn't be rushed.

Beth was feeling stronger by the day, and her only worries, at the moment, were financial. She opened the top drawer of her bureau and found the diamond wedding band she had once cherished. Now it was hidden, unceremoniously, among her socks, and the sight of it gave her a feeling of anxiety. She had to get rid of it for a couple of reasons. She needed the money, and she needed this reminder of her mistake, long gone. Keely knew of a reputable jeweler in the diamond district that bought high-end bobbles. They would stop there, after work, before going to Quench. The money from the ring would pad her bank account and make her feel a little more financially secure.

Keely drove to the diamond district, but there wasn't a parking spot in sight, so Beth hopped out while Keely circled the block. The store was one of many in the area, and Keely, who knew the owner, assured Beth he would treat her right. She was greeted pleasantly by a well-dressed man in his late forties. As she handed over her gorgeous ring, her hands shook slightly in anticipation. Rick, the owner, took his time and looked carefully at each stone through his loupe.

"You say your soon to be ex-husband gave you this as your wedding band?"

"Yes, it was the only genuine thing about him, I have discovered," said Beth scornfully.

"I hate to be the bearer of bad news. These are genuine. Genuine cubic zirconia, that is."

"What! No! No! No! They must be diamonds!" wailed Beth.

"I'm sorry, ma'am. The ring is put together very nicely. It's pretty to look at, but it's only worth about $250. I will buy it for that amount."

"Yes, I may as well sell it," said Beth, stunned.

The transaction was completed, and Beth headed to the door loathing Don like never before. She stood out on the sidewalk and could see Keely approaching from down the street. Keely quickly double-parked, and as Beth got into the car, she burst into tears. Keely had a feeling she knew why Beth was crying and between sobs, Beth confirmed it. She stuffed the few bills into her purse, not bothering to count them nor put them into her wallet. As Keely pulled back into traffic, she reached over and placed her hand on Beth's. Beth looked over at her friend and simply said, "Let's get to Quench. I could use a drink."

"You got it."

The parking lot at the swingers' club was filling up fast. Keely thought it resembled the crowd that would typically gather on a weekend, not a Thursday night. Once inside, it was revealed what the draw was. The Japanese knot master was making an appearance. Beth was not in the mood for sex, but cocktails and some kinky education sounded just about right.

"Tonight's on me," said Keely generously.

"Are you sure, Keely? You've done so much for me already."

"Yes, I'm sure. It's fun to hang out with you. You'll be back on your feet again one of these days. Then you'll owe me a drink."

"If you insist," replied Beth as she put her arm around her friend's waist and they headed to the bar.

Kim Ren's apartment in New York City was as he had left it many months ago. Small, compact, austere with only the things he needed and each of those things in their place. He had been in the city for about half a day. Straight from the airport, he had secretly met with an acquaintance who needed his assistance. From the meeting, he had gone to his apartment spending several hours in meditation and yoga, preparing for the Shibari demonstration at Quench.

The limo driver pulled up to Kim's apartment building just as he exited onto the sidewalk. Sliding into the backseat, he closed his eyes and prepared to center himself on the way to the club. The limo pulled up to the front door, and Ren exited the car at the front steps of Quench. As he approached the door, one of the club's bouncers opened it for him; both men bowed to the other. Rosanna greeted her special guest, and again, each bowed to the other. Without a word, he made his way to the small room where he would change his clothing. He knew his bondage model would be preparing also.

Kim Ren arrived wearing black pants and a black shirt. He only wore black. He changed into a pair of black, Lycra bicycle shorts. He was shirtless and shoe-less, not for vanity but because he could practice his craft more effectively, allowing him the freedom of movement that he required. He had no desire to be naked. He was not there to show off his sinewy, muscular body but to show off his skills. His inky black hair was nearly shoulder length, and he pulled it back into a tight bun anchored at the back of his head.

Word had traveled throughout the club that the knot master had arrived and was preparing. Soon, all four, large, picture windows surrounding the knot room had guests lined up to watch the unusual demonstration. Kim stepped into the glass room, leaving the door open behind him. A microphone hung down from the rafter in the middle of the room to pick up any sounds. He began by standing in the center of the room and bowing to the observers at all four windows. Then he explained the art of Shibari, its origin, its uses and how long he had been practicing. Once he finished the history lesson, his female model arrived.

The first thing anyone noticed was the beautiful kimono that she wore. It was of ivory silk covered with hand-painted, mauve chrysanthemums embellished with genuine gold thread. It was an antique work of art, handmade in Japan, of the finest silk, and given as a gift from Kim. To own such a treasure was considered fortunate indeed, as the garment was considered nearly priceless.

Kim approached his model and bowed with deep

respect. After he reverently removed her kimono, she bowed to him and handed her garb to the waiting Rosanna. Kim then took her long hair and, in a few quick twists, piled it ornately on top of her head, securing it with a piece of silk. From where Beth stood, she could only see the back of the model. She had jet black hair that was poker straight and long enough to tickle the middle of her back. She stood about five feet six inches tall and was very curvaceous with a long torso and matching legs. Physically prepared, the model also bowed to all four windows. As she turned toward her window, Beth could see the woman was not young, around middle-age. He bountiful breasts sagged appropriately, her abdomen protruded slightly, and her curvy hips made her waist look small. As she stood up from her bow, Beth recognized her. It was Lori!

"Why didn't you tell me Lori was his model?"

"I thought it would be a good surprise. He loves Lori's curves and long torso. You'll see why as he progresses." And she did.

The rope was hemp, used for historical and practical purposes. Every knot had historical significance, and the geometric patterns made by the ropes across Lori's body were nothing short of visual art. Her deep curves and smooth skin contrasted beautifully with the texture of the tight ropes. The soft flesh of Lori's hips, buttocks, and breasts squeezed by the ropes created shapes and shadows. Although the pattern ended up to be incredibly intricate, the Nawashi, or knot artist, made it look easy. The uninformed onlooker may have been worried about the welfare of the model; however, Kim had explained that the ropes, when applied correctly, mimicked the effects of acupressure and Shiatsu massage. The whole scenario served to emphasize sensuality, vulnerability, and strength.

As Kim and Lori completed the demonstration, surprisingly, there was no applause as Beth would have expected. The silence served as a sign of respect. Kim then bowed deeply to Lori as a sign of gratitude, then bowed once again to all those watching. At that moment, the lights went out in the glass room, signaling a cue for the onlookers to depart. Once the crowd left, the microphone was turned off and the door closed, Ren removed his shorts to allow his throbbing member some room for expansion. With Lori still encased in ropes, he began to massage her nipples which protruded from between the ropes. The blackness, her vulnerability that she felt from being tied up, yet the sensual nature of Kim made her sexually ready, indeed. She was bound in a standing position with her wrists knotted behind her back and her legs anchored far apart, exposing her pubic area.

Kim's flicking tongue began at her breasts making its way down her torso, hop-scotching between the decorative ropes toward her female triangle stopping at her clit. Like the girls from Tokyo's pink district, who worked on him while he relaxed, it was now his turn to please. His mission was to pamper his woman, and once he knew she was close to orgasm, he deftly released her legs, manipulating her stance and plunged his hard cock into her moist pussy that lay in wait beneath her swollen clitoris. Their coupling was swift and highly effective, serving as a way of bonding between the two.

Now he needed to reverse his knot tying to free Lori, which took less than a minute. In the dark, she recovered her kimono, and Kim assisted her in dressing before he put on his tight shorts. They bowed deeply to each other without conversation. The only word was a quiet *arigato* spoken by the knot master.

Beth and Keely sat at the bar on the main floor following the demonstration.

"What did you think of the whole thing?" asked Keely.

"I've never seen or heard anything like it," admitted Beth. "What is this guy's background? I mean, how do you get into such a thing?"

"His name is Kim Ren, and he is American born. He has lived in Japan for about twenty years and loves the Japanese culture. I hear he has black belts in several of the martial arts."

"I'm not surprised. Did you see the abs on that guy? I don't think he has an ounce of fat on him," remarked Beth.

"Yes, he is gorgeous...and a little mysterious. Once he finishes his demo, he always slinks out of here into a waiting limo, so I've been told. He never socializes at the club or with anyone."

"I think he is incredibly sexy," said Beth.

"You and everyone else who's ever seen him," laughed Keely.

"Is his demo always the same?"

"Yes and no. He always uses Lori, but his knots and knot patterns change. He must know hundreds of knots – it's amazing. Tonight, most of the rope ended up making diamonds down her torso. I hadn't seen that design before."

"What an interesting show, for lack of a better word. I was a little surprised to see Lori on the stage. I thought she would be home with Larry."

As the conversation continued, the women saw Lori walking toward them. Beth couldn't ask Lori enough questions about her experience. But what was really intriguing was what happened after the lights went out.

Beth thought Lori was a lucky girl.

"The sex is a way of thanking each other, but also, there is a lot of sexual tension building as he touches my body while manipulating the ropes. It is the most sensuous thing to ever be a part of. No disrespect to Larry, of course."

"Speaking of Larry, how is he doing?"

"He's doing great. As you know, the doctors have allowed him to go back to work half days. He has lost some weight, and he is feeling stronger and stronger. I wasn't sure I should come tonight, but he insisted that I not disappoint everyone here."

Lori ordered a cocktail, and as they finished sipping their drinks and visiting, they agreed it was time to head home. They would be busy the next day at the bakery.

Chapter 19

The police in Miami had nothing new to tell Beth. She checked in with them occasionally only to learn, each time, they had not located Don and had no new leads. In reality, the police had found Don and were continuing their sting operation. He had been illegally importing and selling knock-off apparel, accessories, and handbags from China for years. They knew he had many people working under him and a few very nasty bosses above him. He was in deep and part of a huge operation. He was not the sharpest knife in the drawer, but was close enough to the kingpins to be worth staking out. Don Lyons, his alias, was sloppy, and if his bosses knew just how stupid the guy was, they would have erased him from the business – permanently. The police were waiting for him to lead them to bigger fish, additional information about the importing ring, so he would implicate more criminals. They weren't only interested in him but also the scores of others he associated with. Soon, very soon, Don Lyons's life would change like never before.

The Miami police weren't the only ones who knew Beth's husband was a problem. Back in Kendrick, Don's fingerprints on the bar glass that Randy had saved revealed some important information. The law enforcement systems had made a match between the fingerprints of Don Lyons and Julio Ramirez, a known criminal from Florida. He had been in trouble with the law and had served a few short sentences for assault, petty theft, fraud and drug possession.

It didn't take long for word to spread throughout Club Climax about Beth's con-man husband. People eventually caught on that the Anderson boys were living with the Wards, and the reason spread like a brush fire. For a brief second, Tom had an "I told you moment" then he only felt rage toward Don and empathy for Beth and her little boys. Tom knew Randy had done some investigating, but so had he. Tom's team had been able to track Don's business dealings as well as his comings and goings. Little did Don realize that the email address he had so innocently shared with Tom had given Tom and his thugs a portal for complete access to his computer. Tom had been obsessed with nailing this guy and knew it was time for his info and Randy's to end up on the same page. Tom's fleet of private eyes didn't always use the most conventional methods of data collecting, but they were highly effective.

The Miami sting operation was a guarded secret. The Feds had spent countless man hours and money on the investigation, so Randy and his department had not been kept in the loop and even Tom's seasoned private eyes, on the street, had heard nothing. Even if Tom had known to back off Don's case, so the Feds could work unencumbered, it wasn't likely he would have changed his tactics. With Beth involved, it was far too personal. Don was going to pay for what he had done to a widow and her children, according to Tom's rules.

Unfortunately, Tom hadn't found out what had happened to Beth until several weeks after Beth had left town. Had she been up front with him, he would have had a better chance of finding Don sooner. By now, the sniveling coward had been given some lead time to get himself lost. But Tom's team all had law enforcement backgrounds, was thorough and had contacts in many major cities, including Miami. Most were retired FBI, Secret Service, and CIA, but none of them had to follow their departments' rules any longer. Getting the job done was all that mattered. How it was carried out and at what cost were factors that Tom never worried about.

Don could hardly believe his eyes when he saw the bank balance in black and white. He now had his hands on several million dollars. Everything had worked out perfectly. Not only had Beth liquidated all her portfolios and deposited the checks into their joint account, but her house had sold at the most opportune time, allowing another $450,000 influx of cash into the same account. The icing on the cake was that he could withdraw it and be gone before she made her way back to Miami. He had made a clean getaway in a small boat he had purchased and headed first to the Keys. From there, he island-hopped into the Caribbean, setting up a bank account in the Cayman Islands, avoiding all customs and immigration along the way. Life was good. It was very, very good. He had all the money he would ever need, and he didn't have to deal with naïve Beth and her brats any longer.

Julio, aka, Don, sat in a quaint restaurant on the quiet east side of Grand Cayman while most tourists were miles away, crowding into the area known as Seven Mile Beach. The restaurant looked like a cheesy tiki bar on the outside, but inside, it was clear that besides a well-stocked bar, it was also available for fine dining. The back deck overlooked the rear of the restaurant and the ocean. Anyone sitting out there would be hidden from other patrons: a good thing for paranoid Don. He sat outside guzzling multiple drinks with several beautiful, college-age women. He was hammered and reveling in their attention, continuing to buy drinks for everyone. He watched some of the staff take a break and appear behind the restaurant, below them. Several waiters lit up cigarettes and sat down on five gallon pails that they turned upside down. One of the chefs from the kitchen appeared and attached a whole chicken to a chain which was anchored up on the beach. Don couldn't figure out what they were doing and finally hollered down to the men.

"What is that for?" he asked, slurring his speech.

The chef who had tethered the meat responded, "We have a shark that comes here every day and eats when we feed him. Watch, you'll see."

Don was most interested in the show and moved unsteadily down the back stairs, to the beach below, away from the beauties who had been hanging all over him. As he approached the bottom step, he yelled, "This I gotta see."

After securing the meat, the chef and a waiter began to swish the ocean water with their hands announcing to the shark that dinner was served. After a couple of minutes, with no reaction, the staff repeated their watery invitation. This time, the shark appeared and, without hesitation, ate the chicken in one gulp. Don had watched numerous television programs on sharks, but seeing the strength and brutality of one up close was frightening.

When the show ended, Don relieved himself in the ocean and turned around to head back up onto the deck where he nearly ran into a woman who had snuck up behind him. It was getting dark, and the glow from the lit torches barely kissed the shoreline.

"Hi," she said.

"Well, hello there," said Don as he eyed her up and down.

She was no older than thirty, with long, brown hair that was whipping around her face from the ocean breeze. She wore a fluorescent pink bikini top that barely contained her large, tanned breasts, and a bright floral sarong tied loosely around her shapely hips.

"Do you really think you should be walking alone out here?" Don asked her.

"I'm not alone, now, am I?" she teased.

"Are you looking for company?" asked Don, boldly.

"I saw you earlier, at the bar. You look like an actor. Has anyone ever told you that?" she asked moving closer to him, so her right breast, with its stiff nipple, brushed his left arm. Don could smell the aroma of marijuana coming from her hair and alcohol on her breath.

"Yes, I've been told I look like Don Johnson, actually."

She placed one hand on the back of his neck and the other on the back of his head, drawing him to her. She kissed him hard and met no resistance. Her tongue was smooth and moist and jockeyed for position within his mouth. He kissed her back with the same fervor, fully aroused from the warmth of her mouth, the softness of her lips, and the feel of her boobs pressing against his chest.

He brought up his right hand and, despite his buzz, deftly pulled the string to her bikini top, freeing her breasts into his welcoming hands. He pushed his thumbs into her nipples, causing her to moan. She threw back her head and arched her back – offering her gifts to his eager mouth. He sucked both nipples in turn, teasing her with the tip of his flicking tongue and tips of his fingers.

She pushed Don away, untied her sarong, and pulled off her bikini bottoms.

"Fuck me in the sand as the tide comes in," she

demanded.

Don pulled off his t-shirt and shed his board shorts. She was lying in the sand, facing the ocean, spread eagle, allowing the water to tickle her snatch. With his flag at full-staff, he knelt between her legs and inserted two fingers into her pussy. He wiggled them in and out, enjoying his mystery partner's moans and watching her thrust her pelvis toward him. With his other hand, he thumbed her clit in a circular motion until she grabbed his forearm.

"Stop! I'm going to cum! Fuck me!"

Don lay on top of her and, grabbing his cock, forced himself inside her hot pussy. He could feel the warm ocean water crashing against their genitals with every thrust. He ran his tongue over her full, open lips before covering her mouth with his. He grabbed her hair and kissed her hungrily, and she did the same to him. Their pelvis's rocked together in unison until he felt her tight vaginal walls shudder around the spams of his cock.

"Ahh, ahh," was all she could say as she panted and caught her breath.

"Oh, my God, you're so hot, baby," said Don, kissing her lightly before rolling off and enjoying the warm surf that was licking them around their waists. He closed his eyes for a few minutes, catching his breath as he enjoyed the ocean breeze. He opened his eyes and turned to find out, how and when, he could fuck this beauty again, only to discover she had vanished.

Maybe it was just as well. He didn't need to get to know anyone, nor did he want anyone getting familiar with him. He had thought this beautiful oasis was as good a place as any to lay low temporarily, but he knew he needed to leave this country, altogether, and get to a busy metropolis where he would have a better chance of blending in. He had heard Ecuador was a great place to live. It had a good standard of living, and he could speak the native language. Several more days on Grand Cayman seemed just about right. Sun, surf, and women mingled with Mai Tai's and Margaritas was how a millionaire should live. He got drunk daily, smoked some exceptional weed often, and bought a plane ticket to Ecuador.

Don was traveling very light. He would buy everything brand new once he arrived at his destination. He had cleaned up well and was wearing some clothes that actually made him look like he had money. Don stood out from the other passengers. His new threads were very dapper; the wedding suit that Beth had so generously paid for was the perfect choice. The accompanying shirt and tie screamed expensive and was only over-shadowed by the Panama hat that sat pompously on his head, slightly angled to give him swag.

Don sat with his back against the wall at gate 12 waiting to board his flight. The plane was at the gate and had deplaned its passengers. The only thing holding up the boarding process was the re-fueling, cleaning, and re-stocking of the plane for the flight to South America. Don crossed his legs, leaned his head back against the wall, and closed his eyes with a smirk on his face. There was no time for a proper siesta, but this was the first time today he had been able to relax. It was his false sense of security that allowed him to let down his guard and miss seeing the two men in dark suits approaching. They stood directly in front of him drawing all kinds of attention from everyone except from the man they were there to apprehend.

When their presence provoked no reaction, the man on the left nudged Don's knee with his own. Don briefly opened his eyes expecting to see the person whose suitcase had just hit his leg but instead was surprised to see two men peering down at him.

"You Don Lyons?" asked one of the men.

"No, you got the wrong guy."

"Really? I guess you'd rather be known as Julio Ramirez, then."

Realizing he had been found out, he quickly admitted his identity and indignantly asked why they cared. Ignoring his question, the man simply answered, "You're coming with us."

Before Don could get another word out, they had yanked him to his feet, spun him around, placed his hands behind his back and had tightly zip tied his wrists together. The two men fit the profiles of police officers right down to their ability to cuff their suspect quickly and smoothly. The only person in the boarding area who didn't believe they were cops was Don. His disbelief stemmed not because they weren't convincing, but because he knew there were others out looking for him who would be more efficient and ruthless. Don began to pray these guys were the police.

Each man grabbed an elbow and led Don out of the airport to a waiting black town car. These guys were quick, efficient, organized and determined. They weren't the cops.

"Hey, c'mon guys, you don't have to do this. I can pay you whatever you want –in cash– to just let me disappear. I can have the money in your hands in half an hour." Now things were getting real. Don continued, "You could both be wealthy and never have to work again." With no reaction whatsoever from his captors, Don's voice cracked as he tried to keep from crying. When trying to pay them off didn't work, he resorted to begging. Neither man spoke a word. The gig was up. Don was scared shitless.

Chapter 20

Living in New York City had become mundane. The glitz of the big city that Beth had felt as a tourist had fizzled out. Now, the city felt like just a place to make a living. She had little time, energy, and even less money to see the sights or venture away from her neighborhood. Beth had been in New York several months and had yet to make it back to Kendrick. She had worked every shift faithfully and had taken as much overtime as she was offered. At first, she missed her boys, calling them several times a day, trying to stay connected. But now, she called only a few times a week, and each time she spoke with them, they sounded happy but always anxious to end their conversation with her. It hurt her feelings a little, but she was relieved that they were doing well.

Beth's money was tight. The cost of living in the city was incredibly high. She felt like she was on a treadmill, working hard but not getting anywhere. She had little extra money to treat herself. Her hair extensions were gone, she hadn't been able to afford a manicure, and makeup couldn't conceal the dark circles under her eyes or the wrinkles brought on by worry and fatigue. She was a lost soul in a huge metropolis hanging on by a thread.

As the months went by, Beth began to adopt an "I don't give a shit" attitude. Life had screwed her over several times, and she was done being Miss Goody Two

Shoes. From now on, she would do what made Beth happy and worry less about others. She had latched onto a group of hardcore rockers. Their alternative music was as annoying as their alternative decorum. As open-minded as Keely was, she tried to discourage Beth from befriending the group. They were known drug users and into a lot of kink, and Keely worried that Beth's current frame of mind could blur her good judgment.

Beth's one constant was Quench. If Keely wasn't heading to the club, Beth would get a member friend to pick her up. Although it was a swingers' club, there were rules and etiquette to follow. Individual couples had their own codes of conduct, but Beth seemed to feel she could be the exception. She had been known to text some of her club hookups asking to meet them outside Quench. Complaints, such as this and others compounded and more than once, Rosanna had to talk to Beth in private, threatening her with club expulsion unless she began to play nice. Some of Beth's avant-garde behavior had spilled over into her job, as well.

Larry had made several friendly comments regarding her appearance and her attitude, hoping to get the message across without being confrontational. But when that proved ineffective, and Beth began showing up late for work due to hangovers and late nights, a more direct approach was necessary. Larry called her into his office and made it clear she needed to improve on several levels or she would lose her job. He reminded her that although they were sympathetic to her plight, they had a business to run.

Beth was embarrassed. She had never been reprimanded on the job. She knew she had an attitude and personality change and couldn't disagree with Larry altogether. She began to pay more attention to her appearance and went to a discount salon for a haircut. She had cleaned up enough to pass Larry's inspection at the job, but on her days off, she hung out with the band.

Keely never knew when, or if, Beth was coming home, and if she did, who she would drag home with her and just how stoned or drunk they would be. Beth's living style began to wear on Keely's nerves, and she ended up having to set some ground rules. Things improved temporarily when one of Beth's new friends was found dead of a drug overdose with the needle still stuck between his toes. It was sobering for Beth, giving her pause. With this improved behavior, Keely, Larry, and Lori left her alone but remained unimpressed by many of her decisions.

Beth's new friends had introduced her to sex outside of Quench. Their group had been invited to an old fashioned key party – something that swingers had indulged in decades before. The party was held at the private estate of the member of a world famous rock band who had retired from playing. Despite his age, he still enjoyed playing the persona of a rock star, complete with drugs, booze, women and sex, much to the delight of his groupies.

Tristan Branneth opened the arched, oak front door to his old, stone mansion. He had already buzzed open the wrought iron gate when Beth had announced herself through the intercom. As the door opened, her cab sped away, and she walked up the Omni-stone walkway to the towering home. Tristan's estate featured what appeared to be a mini castle, complete with turrets at the end of two wings. Half of the walls of the mansion were covered in ivy, and the perfectly trimmed lawns and meandering English-style flower beds would had fooled many a passerby into thinking the owner was a distinguished professor or heir to a conglomerate fortune.

Even tonight, the cars parked in the drive did not give away a thing. Two Bentleys, a Mercedes, a Porsche, a Viper and too many BMWs to count lined both sides of the circular driveway. The windows on the first floor were well lit, and '80s rock music was blasting through the overhead speaker system, flooding the expansive, hedge-rimmed yard and the street on the other side.

Tristan had not aged well; his stringy, dyed blonde hair hung limply below his thin shoulders, and the wrinkles in his face looked etched in stone. His tired, blue eyes, normally dull, were already glazed over. Too many drug-filled decades laced with alcohol and hot, young women eager to spread their legs for this British rock legend had taken its toll.

"Beth, welcome!" said Tristan as he planted a kiss on her lips.

"Hi, Tristan. Thank you for inviting me."

"Come in, come in. Robert will take your coat."

As if he were x-raying her, his eyes ran up and down Beth's body. She had hoped her black, Bordelle Bandage Dress and Christian Louboutin pumps were appropriate for a party such as this. She hadn't worn this dress since the swinger's cruise, the night she fell in love with Don. She couldn't dwell on that or the night when Tom had presented her with the dress at their penthouse love nest. It all felt like ages ago.

Beth knew it was a swingers' party but still worried that she wouldn't fit in with the wealthy friends that Tristan hung out with. She took extra care with her makeup, concealing the dark circles under her eyes and playing up her full lips with a shiny, red lip gloss. Her short, brown hair was moussed, giving it a sexy, tousled appearance. The dress pushed up her boobs, cinched in her waist, and the cut-out showed off her still shapely rump.

Grabbing the cut crystal bowl from the ornate, mahogany, foyer table, Tristan asked Beth to drop in her car keys. She looked into the bowl, which contained multiple sets of keys on a variety of key chains.

"I didn't drive my car here," lied Beth, who didn't have a car in the city. "I took a cab."

"No worries, luv. I'll make sure you get a hookup."

He placed his hand on Beth's right ass cheek and escorted her down the hall to the expansive dining hall. Beth couldn't believe the spread of food that lay on the beautifully decorated fifty-foot table. It was covered with tempting hors d'oeuvres, including caviar. Stuffed turkeys, prime rib, assorted side dishes and sumptuous desserts filled the rest of the table except where the lit candelabras sat. The room was so cavernous that the huge table did not fill it, and there was still room for a long marble-topped, mahogany wet bar in the corner.

A sexy, young woman dressed as a Playboy Bunny stood behind the bar obviously having problems pouring the drinks, but no one seemed to mind her incompetence. The area dwarfed the mere twenty or thirty guests nibbling on the feast before them while they sipped mixed drinks or sparkling bubbly. The women were dressed in short, sexy cocktail dress, and most of the men chose slacks with button-down shirts or turtleneck sweaters. The ages were mixed; about half were Beth's age, the other half younger. Tristan was definitely the most senior person at the party. Beth recognized a few people but in a hazy way. She had spent a lot of time in an altered state with the band and Tristan's friends.

"Help yourself to food, and over there, Vicki will make you a drink or pour you some champagne," said Tristan.

"And don't forget to check out the candy table." Beth knew Tristan was referring to an array of drugs: methamphetamine, cocaine, heroin, marijuana, GHB and Ecstasy. All were beautifully displayed near the entrance to the dining room on a large side table. The contrast of the visually appealing drug display and the ugliness of the drugs' consequences was not lost on Beth.

"Thanks, Tristan," said Beth.

"Catch you later, honey," he replied as he darted to the front door once again.

Beth found her way to Vicki and quickly downed one glass of champagne to steady her nerves. Then she asked for a second. She headed to the drug table, perused the selection, thinking it would help her to forget her life for just a little while.

"Need some help deciding?" said a man from behind.

Beth turned to face the man whose hand was now on the small of her back. The first thing she noticed, besides the deep timber of his voice, was that he smelled delicious – she would have to ask him later what cologne he was wearing. He stood taller than Beth, approximately five feet ten inches. His perfectly tailored, gray, Italian designer suit hugged his slight build. He had wavy, brown hair and a closely trimmed beard and mustache that matched his hair color exactly. His piercing, gray-green eyes were surrounded by thick black lashes that sat above his pointed, hawk-shaped nose. He suggestively licked his somewhat full lips as Beth took in his features.

"Hi. I'm Ellis."

"Nice to meet you. I'm Beth," she said as she extended her right hand to shake his.

"Have you been to a key party before?" asked Ellis.

"No, I haven't. I took a cab here tonight because I thought the weather might get bad, so I'm not sure how it will work out for me," said Beth with a nervous laugh.

"I'll be glad to be your date since I'm staying here tonight," said Ellis, with a wink. *Why not?* thought Beth.

"Deal, unless you get a better offer from one of the younger girls."

"You can hold your own, I would wager," replied Ellis. "How about a few lines of coke? And you'll need one of these, too," said Ellis as he held up a small green tablet with a shamrock stamped on it. Recognizing Ecstasy, Beth opened her mouth and allowed Ellis to place it on her tongue.

"Bottoms up," she said as she drained her glass of champagne. Following suit, Ellis swallowed his pill, then cut up a few lines of coke on the glass mirror that was so thoughtfully provided. He held the tube to Beth's nose, and inhaling deeply, she snorted a line of the fine white powder up each nostril. Mimicking Beth's action, Ellis did the same.

"Let's dance," invited Ellis, dragging her from the dining hall into the spacious living room. Beth looked at the cathedral ceiling dripping with crystal chandeliers hanging from heavy, wooden beams. The small-paned picture windows screamed Tudor, and the heavy maroon draperies with dangling gold tassels affirmed the vintage look. The decorator had gone Tudor all the way. Her love of design prompted Beth to look far more at the décor than at her dancing partner.

The furniture consisted of multiple, dark brown, leather couches sporting dozens of tufted buttons. The chairs looked far more welcoming and cozy. Their design was wingback, and they were covered in a heavy, flowered Damask fabric featuring maroon, deep blue, dark green with gold thread outlining each flower. Most of the furniture was huddled around the great stone fireplace that took up a good portion of the room's side wall. On the other side of the room were several, small group seatings. High back, carver chairs sat on either side of a handmade tea table. Another seating group of six chairs sat next to a round table that held a chess set. The table, chairs, and chess set were beautiful yet very rustic. Beth was sure they were all original period pieces that would be worth far more than her year's salary. The entire space was covered with highly-polished wide plank oak flooring. Each of the seating areas was anchored by very expensive tightly woven area rugs. Each rug was the same and only varied in size and shape. The rich, dark colors of the wool mimicked the colors in the room's drapes and chairs.

For a contemporary rocker, Beth wondered why Tristan would chose such an antiquated look for his home. The only thing she could come up with was that because his heritage was British, his house served to remind him of home.

Ellis and Beth danced alongside several other couples, while consuming more and more champagne that Vicki offered from a silver serving tray. Feeling euphoric and slow dancing to "Freebird" made Beth giggle.

"I feel like I am at a middle-school dance," she laughed. Ellis kissed her, sliding his tongue into Beth's mouth and moving his hands over her ass, cupping and kneading her cheeks through the crisscross fabric of her dress. Beth eagerly kissed him back, wanting to be fucked right in front of everyone. She wasn't in middle school anymore! She was just about to suggest finding an empty bedroom when Tristan dimmed the lights slightly and turned down the music.

"I hope you're all having a good time!" shouted Tristan. "And I hope you've had a chance to eat and mingle and get to know some people. But the hour is late, and it's time to pick out a set of keys!" His guests hollered, hooted, clapped and whistled in response.

"Okay, one half of each couple, line up and grab a set of keys."

Beth watched as all the highly attractive guests approached Tristan and, with their hand over their eyes, reached inside the bowl and held up a set of car keys. The men and women, eager to see who their fuck buddy was for the rest of the night, gave a cat-call and walked with their partner to get their coats and leave. The ladies kissed and said goodbye to their husbands or partners before leaving the rustic mansion.

Tristan's keys were also in the bowl and held high by a young blonde *with fake everything* mused Beth. Ellis's Viper keys were held up by an exotic looking, thirty-ish woman with long, straight, black hair, olive complexion, green eyes and large breasts. She wore a red, silk, sheath dress that clung to every curve and left little to the imagination.

"Be right back," said Ellis to Beth as he walked up to the woman and whispered something into her ear. Beth couldn't hear what had been said, but the woman smiled and nodded her head. Ellis walked hand in hand with his new lady friend toward where Beth was standing. With his free hand, he clasped Beth's, and it was clear it was going to be a threesome if she still wanted to be fucked.

"Beth, this is Camila. She's going to join us this evening."

When all the keys were claimed, the party quickly ended, and Tristan led his female companion upstairs. Ellis followed Tristan, still holding Beth and Camila's hands as they walked up the carpeted grand staircase to the second floor. Beneath them was the sound of scurrying as the house staff, out of nowhere, began to clean up the mess the partiers had carelessly left behind.

Ellis had obviously stayed at Tristan's before. He knew his way around and led the girls down the dimly lit hallway to one of the nine bedrooms. More pills and cocaine were available with a variety of alcohol on the mini bar near the fireplace. Ellis turned on the gas-fed fire casting a warm glow and flickering light across the king-size bed and upholstered chaise. Camila popped a few pills, as did Ellis. Beth went for the cocaine and poured herself a stiff Scotch and water, draining the burning liquid in one swig.

Ellis walked over to the bed and began undressing himself, throwing his clothes haphazardly onto the nearby chaise. He climbed up onto the four poster bed and made himself comfortable against the multitude of ornate throw pillows. Camila walked over to Beth and kissed her gently on the lips before probing her tongue inside. Beth pulled her lips away, having another move in mind. Bending downwards, Beth grasped the hem of Camila's silk chemise, pulled it over her head, revealing she had nothing on underneath. Beth kicked off her shoes and turned her back to Camila. Camila took the hint, and unzipped her bandage dress, slowly pulling it down to the floor.

Keeping her eyes on Ellis, Beth felt Camila's breasts, belly, and pelvis push up against her back. Camila reached around Beth, cupping her breasts and finding her nipples. She tweaked, pulled, and rolled them between her fingers while Beth tilted her head back showing her appreciation of Camila's efforts. Beth leaned her head back onto Camila's shoulder and turned to kiss her once again. Camila removed her right hand from Beth's breast and found her pussy. Spreading her stance, she allowed Camila to push her probing fingers into her pussy, warm and wet with desire. Beth turned to her and began suckling her large, dark nipple surrounded by a luscious, chocolate-looking areola.

Camila nudged Beth backward until she felt the bed behind her knees and sat down. Camila moved between Beth's legs and knelt down pushing Beth's legs wider apart. Ellis could not sit still and just watch any longer. Nothing made him hornier than watching a woman eating out another woman. Ellis crawled from the head of the bed and, still facing the women, straddled Beth's mouth shoving his long, throbbing cock into her mouth, which she greedily accepted. Continuing to watch girl on girl was intensifying the excellent head that Beth was giving him.

Beth swirled her tongue around his cock and sucked while Ellis pumped in and out of her mouth. He removed his cock every few strokes, so Beth could lick his nads, before gently sucking and rolling them around in her hot, warm mouth. Beth could hardly concentrate on sucking Ellis off thanks to Camila's asp-like tongue darting in and out of her vagina. She had spread wide, encouraging Camila to lick every inch of her vulva and clitoris, which Camila had happily done, exploring her womanhood with the length and tip of her tongue and entire mouth.

Beth felt herself cuming and gripped the bedspread with tight fists as she arched her pelvis up and down toward Camila's greedy mouth. Her moans were muffled by Ellis's cock, which immediately released its load down Beth's throat, unable to hold back any longer. Beth lay gasping and enjoying her post-orgasmic state along with the Ecstasy-cocaine-alcohol buzz she was feeling. She was barely aware of Ellis and Camila fucking beside her on the bed before everything went dark.

Beth had felt honored to be invited along and, despite

being older than her friends, tried twice as hard to fit in by indulging more than anyone else. When her group could not wake her up to go home, they left her there. In the morning, she woke up in the rocker's house, naked in a strange bed. Although she had no recollection of having sex, she knew she had been violated mysteriously. Her very sore vulvar area and vaginal bleeding were not indicators of normal sexual activity. She felt swollen between her legs, and if she could get her hands on a small mirror, she was sure she would see bruises. It was obvious her friends didn't give a damn about her. Time to make new friends. Whatever had happened to her, she had told no one about it. She was so ashamed of herself for her recent behavior. She had let her partying dominate her life to the point of total disregard for her kids. She could hardly look at herself in the mirror, she felt so sickened. She needed to own up to her recent failures and make amends.

One day, after work, Beth asked to meet with Larry, Lori, and Keely. The trio of owners didn't know what to expect and wondered if Beth was about to resign. But what she had in mind was quite the opposite. Instead, she apologized for having let them down and for her bad choices. She vowed to take her job more seriously. The next conversation was with Jack, Cindy, and her boys. She set up a call and Skype schedule, determined to keep in better touch with her family. Although the Wards knew nothing of the wild path she had temporarily gone down, they were pleased to hear that they would talk to her more often.

The one thing that Beth did not let up on was Quench. The only reason Keely accompanied Beth to Quench was so that her friend could gain admittance. There was no doubt that Keely did not feel close to Beth these days. Her recent actions had alienated Keely and, while they were out socially together, Keely needed distance from her roommate. Before going their own separate ways, they had agreed on a time they would leave the club, no exceptions.

Beth headed for the first floor bar and couldn't help but notice the stink eye Rosanna gave her at the entrance. Was the attitude contagious? It was the same look Maggie had given her when she took her drink order. *Fuck them both. They think they are better than me,* thought Beth. She had just started sipping her champagne when a familiar voice, and a familiar cologne scent, approached from behind. *Ellis!*

"Hi, babe," said Ellis.

"Thank God, someone without attitude," replied Beth. Ellis raised his eyebrows and Beth continued, "Never mind." She had no desire to go into a long discussion; she was here to fuck. She would even fuck Ellis although she was still unsure what had happened to her at Tristan's party and who was to blame.

"Want to find a room?" asked Ellis.

"Absolutely," said Beth as she pushed away from the bar. Ellis led Beth down the hallway past the Furries Room to the Pirate's Cove on the left.

There was a mini-gang plank that led into the ship themed room that boasted a wooden ship's wheel and a round bed perched up in an elevated crow's nest. Pirate's gear including swords, cat-o-nine-tails, eye patches, boots and breeches hung on rusted hooks on the wall. Ruffled wench skirts, torn peasant blouses, corsets and lace-up boots hung inside the open closet next to the round port window that was lit with a light bulb illuminating faux ocean scenery.

"Ahoy, me maties," said Ellis with a grin.

"Do you want me to dress like a wench for you?" teased Beth.

"No. Just act like one," said Ellis, with a wink.

Beth dropped to her knees and unzipped Ellis's trousers while he pulled off his gray, ribbed turtleneck. He stepped out of his shoes and pants while Beth began pumping his long, narrow cock. He wrapped his fingers throughout Beth's short hair, forcing her head back and forth, several times making her gag as he slipped too far down the back of her throat.

"Lick my balls," he commanded, as Beth sucked them alternatively inside her hot mouth, gliding her tongue over his wrinkled, hairless ball sac. Ellis, feeling like he was going to cum already, backed away from his little wench.

"Let's get these clothes off you," he said, nearly tearing off her blue silk blouse. Beth pushed his hands away gently from the pearl buttons and deftly unbuttoned herself. She didn't bother wearing a bra or panties, which Ellis obviously approved of by whistling as he pulled off her black, pencil skirt. Now naked, Beth turned to climb the four stairs to the crow's nest bed, covered in a navy blue bedspread. Climbing the stairs right behind her, Ellis slapped Beth's ass cheek causing a red welt to instantly appear.

"Stay on your hands and knees when you get up there."

"Yes, captain," laughed Beth. She got into position and felt the sting of Ellis's hand on her rump several more times.

"Yea, slap my ass hard!" Beth said encouragingly.

"Do you want me to fuck you hard?" asked Ellis, now fully turned on.

"Yes! Fuck my pussy hard!"

Ellis stuffed his cock deep into Beth's wet pussy while

his balls slapped at her thighs with every thrust. To go deeper, Beth rocked her hips and ass toward him with every stroke. Ellis marveled at her full, round ass and gripped it hard, feeling the cushion of Beth's cheeks envelope him. In their frenzied fucking, his cock, wet from Beth's juices, slipped from her pussy and drove hard into her anus. Meeting no objection, he continued to pound at her wiggling ass. The smaller and tighter orifice provided more delicious friction, and he knew he was going to cum and cum hard, so he pulled out of her ass and back into the looser walls of Beth's juicy cunt. Reaching down, he stroked her clit a few times when he felt her pussy walls surround his cock in her own orgasm.

"Fuck, yeah," he said as he grunted out his own orgasm, filling Beth up with his hot spunk in several hard thrusts. "You are one hell of a fuck," said Ellis as he slapped Beth's ass lightly and collapsed beside her.

"Yeah, that's me all right," said Beth, lying down on her side facing away from him.

Keely wasn't in the mood for sex. In fact, since Larry's heart attack, she rarely wanted to come to the club anymore. She even scared herself a little when thoughts of monogamy and a real relationship instead of endless casual sex popped into her head. She loved sex as much as the next girl – but she wanted more. She needed to talk to her best friend, Aaron. Because of their long friendship dating back to their elementary school days in Pittsburgh, he was the one person who knew her better than anyone. Aaron had texted her earlier that day saying he would be at Quench. She needed to find him. He worked in Manhattan as a fashion magazine editor and still took some modeling assignments here and there. He didn't have a lot of free time, so Keely was glad she could touch base with him tonight.

She knew he would be in the Glory Hole. It was a themed room for gay men only, but all voyeurs were welcome. Aaron was an exhibitionist at heart and wouldn't mind Keely watching him. He had tried watching Keely having sex with a man once, a long time ago, but it was so weird that he had left the room. They still had a good laugh over it when they got drunk and reminisced about the "old days."

Keely opened the door to the room, and there he was. *Such a good looking guy. What a waste*, she thought. Aaron was sitting naked on a stool facing a partial wall that was about seven feet tall and approximately fifteen feet long. Round holes four inches in diameter were cut into the wall every three feet with a padded, leather stool beneath. Aaron's mouth was wrapped around a rather large, erect cock that jutted through one of the openings in the wall. He was working the cock with his watering mouth alternating with his eager hand. Keely couldn't see who the recipient was, and she had no idea if Aaron knew him either. The room was set up so men could come and go on both sides of the wall anonymously, but could also hookup on one side of the room, if agreeable. The other side of the wall was a mirror image of where Aaron sat. It also contained a queen-size bed and a bathroom with toilet, sink, shower and a good supply of mouthwash, toothbrushes and toothpaste.

Aaron's hand job was becoming more vigorous when Keely noticed fresh cum spurting out from the mystery cock, landing all over Aaron's face. She watched him lick a drop of man milk that was trickling down near the corner of his mouth. The other man pressed his mouth against the opening where his cock had just exploded, and the two men shared a deep kiss.

Standing up, Aaron saw Keely and rushed over to her. He attempted to kiss her on the cheek, but Keely held him at arm's length and laughingly said, "Oh no, you go wash your face and use some mouthwash first."

"Oh, my God, yaassss!"

Keely watched him prance to the bathroom, not a hair out of place, as usual. He wore his hair shaved on both sides, and his bleached blonde pompadour on top stood several inches high.

"Come in here and talk to me, girlfriend," Aaron beckoned. Keely walked to the doorway, and thankfully, he had already put on his pants. "What's up with you?" he asked, but before she had time to answer he continued, "That beast gave me a hell of a blowjob before you came in. We are meeting at the third floor bar for drinks later, then hopefully back to his place. But I told him I must talk with my best friend before any of that!" said Aaron, emphatically. Aaron continued to dress and talk about himself until Keely thought he forgot why she was even standing in the Glory Hole in the first place. "Let's get a drink and talk about you!" he said, finally.

Keely followed him out of the room as four men came in and jumped onto the bed, starting to pull off one another's clothes. *Perfect timing*, thought Keely. *I wonder how Beth is doing.*

Since being single, Beth had stepped up her sensual side. She could no longer be considered anything but a seasoned and adventurous swinger. She was no longer the sex partner who preferred the blinds down and the door closed. As long as it was legal, she was willing to try it, earning the new title of sex nymph.

Chapter 21

The town car sped through the Grand Cayman city of George Town to the opposite side of the island. Don was confused. He thought they would have taken him back to Miami, which meant staying at the airport. After all, Miami was where his bosses were, and he figured this was a business-related matter. He knew that someday he would get caught skimming a couple thousand off the books each month.

Instead, the three were driven to a small marina where they sped out to sea in a good-sized motor boat. The Caymans, composed of three islands, had varying numbers of residents. They were headed to Little Cayman, which was mostly undeveloped, housing under two hundred witnesses. The boat took a while to reach the small island, enough time for Don to panic.

Eventually, the engine of the boat began to slow down, and in front of them was a beautiful pink beach flanked by tropical lushness. Another man was waiting on the beach to catch the rope that was thrown to him. He quickly grabbed the line and pulled the boat farther up on the sand. Don was ordered off the boat. The rocking of the vessel, coupled with his inability to use his arms, caused Don to fall out of the boat, landing on his stomach in several inches of water. How fortuitous for his captors. They could use his body as a bridge from the boat to the dry sand, enabling them to keep their expensive, Italian leather shoes relatively dry. Once both men literally walked all over him, he struggled to his knees, spitting out sea water and sand. Then, he hoisted himself up on his feet. His beautiful, custom-made suit, now waterlogged, only served to weigh him down. As if the two men were only the delivery boys, they handed him over to the lone man who had awaited them. The two men from the boat disappeared into the trees, seemingly on a mission. As he watched the suits walk away, Don began to have hope. *This might not end so badly. I should be able to hold my own with just one guy.* And that was his last conscious thought. Then the lights went out.

Strange as it may sound, the assassin had no desire to torture his victim. Cleanly snuffing out a piece of garbage was one thing, but making another human being horrendously suffer was another. But the paying client wanted Don to feel pain in retaliation for his crimes, so the suits were back for a little fun. It took some time for Don to wake up out of his unconscious state, which had been induced by a well-placed martial arts kick to the head. Then it took another couple of minutes for him to fully come out of a daze and realize just how bad his situation was. Once his vision cleared up, his heart sank and his flight response kicked in. Trying to scramble to his feet, he ended up back on his ass. His equilibrium had been impaired by the blow to his head, but more effective had been the kick in the ribs he had just received.

"Umph," he involuntarily blurted as he felt bile rise up from his stomach before he hit the ground, hard! Staying where he landed seemed like the best option as far as his ribs were concerned. Looking up from the ground, he managed to breathlessly say, "What the fuck is going on here?"

This time the blow from the suit's shoe hit his nuts. Doubling over in pain, he began to vomit the foul-tasting bile that had been stuck in his throat. The retching caused sharp pains in his lower right ribs, and he knew at least one of them had been broken.

Reeling from the excruciating pain in his scrotum, he managed to get to his knees as he heard the answer to his question. "Somebody doesn't like you and has paid us a lot of money to show you just how much you've pissed him off."

"Guys, guys, you don't have to do this," Don pleaded again. "I have lots of money. I can pay you to stop this."

"You ain't got as much money as our boss has, and you ain't got no power neither. Sorry, you lose," said the thug as his expensive Italian loafer met Don's nose, breaking it and his right eye socket in several places. Immediately a fountain of rich, red blood oozed from both nostrils while the eye began to swell instantly. Don began to lose consciousness again and, as if to wake him up, the paid thugs delivered a couple more blows to his ribs, causing one to puncture his lung near his heart.

"Enough fellas," demanded the assassin. "I will take over from here. Please help me tie him up and get the rope around his neck." Don was unconscious now and did not feel his ankles being shackled by ropes. Nor did he feel a rope being tied around his neck. The cold water of the ocean brought him back to the brink of awareness, but he was too injured and weak to care about what was about to happen. His bruised, battered, and bleeding body was tied to a heavy iron weight, then to the back of the same boat, which had carried him to the island. The three men stepped into the motorboat and idled it away from the beautiful tropical sand beach. Once they hit the throttle and the boat sped toward the open ocean, the noose around Don's neck grew tighter and tighter until he hung to death. Glancing around to be sure no tourists or fishing boats were in sight, the rope tying Don's body to the boat was cut with one slash from a razor sharp knife. His body began to sink without bubbles coming to the surface. Several sharks smelled the fresh blood immediately and came like a fired torpedo to the body's vicinity, but after one bite they swam away, mistakenly thinking the flesh was alive.

Chapter 22

The Christmas season was soon approaching. Thanksgiving was in another week, but the two holidays weren't far apart. Beth had been dreading this time of year. It was not how, or where, she was supposed to be living with two little boys. As was the bakery's annual tradition, the staff had Thanksgiving weekend off giving them a break before the holiday season rush. The owners knew Beth hadn't been home since beginning to work for them due to finances, so as a bonus, they presented her with a round trip plane ticket to Kendrick. She had shrieked with joy and had grabbed and hugged each of them in turn as she comprehended the generosity of her friends, once again. There was only a couple of days before her trip, and she had saved enough money to buy a few inexpensive Christmas gifts that she would take with her. She knew she would not be with the boys for Christmas but was well aware that it was a sacrifice worth making.

She had called her friends to tell them of her upcoming trip, and they encouraged her to plan an evening at Climax. There, she could visit with many of her friends in one place, at one time. She left New York Wednesday after work, going straight to LaGuardia.

Jack, Cindy, and the boys were waiting at the Kendrick airport for her when she landed. The boys obviously remembered her, but both seemed guarded.

They each hugged her, but it was the kind of hug reserved for a great aunt; someone you don't really know – a duty hug. Beth noticed the awkwardness but was sure they would warm up to her by the following day. She stayed with Jack and Cindy, and two nights later they went to Climax for the evening.

Each time Tom had returned to Climax, he had had a private conversation with Randy regarding the search for Don. Each time, there had been no news until now. Tom was cautious as he chose his words. Although Randy was on his side, he was still a cop, sworn to uphold the law. Most of Climax's patrons had moved away from the bar to the dance floor, outdoor hot tub, or playrooms. Tom slid onto a seat at the far end, so they could have some privacy. Randy knew the signal. He filled the glasses of those waiting first, then brought Tom a double of single malt Scotch.

"What's up, brother?" asked Randy.

"I heard Don Lyons made an appearance, then a disappearance – for good."

"You don't say," responded Randy.

"Well, you know how rumors get started. Might be true might not be," said Tom as he stared straight ahead while taking a sip of the liquor.

"Did the rumor mill say where this disappearance happened?"

"I might have heard it was in the Caribbean, kind of sounded like Cayman – or I may have overheard it wrong," replied Tom, coyly.

"That is interesting, my friend."

The clues Tom had relayed to Randy were more than enough. All Randy would say was that someone had left an anonymous tip, and he was merely relaying the information. Within hours, the Cayman Island police force were scouring each of the three islands. They had traced Don to the airport, had taken a statement from the gate agent about a man being led away in handcuffs before he could board his plane to Ecuador. His fake identification showed a different name, but the description the airline worker provided matched Don perfectly. When the police showed his mug shot to the worker, she verified their suspicion. She had attempted to describe the two men, whom she believed to be police officers, but there was nothing remarkable to tell.

It took only days for the police dive team to find the body. When they dragged it to the surface and into the police boat, they were intrigued. The victim was tied up as expected, but the unique rope knots were something they had not seen before. The body was quickly identified through DNA and shipped back to Miami. The Miami police were disappointed in Julio Ramirez's death. He had been a stepping stone to much bigger fish. Once they looked through the file, they could see no reason to keep his death quiet, and Beth received the call while in Kendrick. She was surprised that she felt mixed feelings about the news. She thought she would have been overjoyed, but instead she felt grief all over again. Maybe she had held out hope that Don would have come to his senses, come back with her money, and want to build the life that they had planned. Now, his demise meant the death of that dream once and for all.

The good news was now they might be able to find her money. The police agreed they would investigate tracing the funds. Because the body was found in the Cayman Islands, it was logical to think he had opened an account there. Sure enough! It was all there! They also found another legal document in the bank's safety deposit box. The will left all his belongings to his wife – good news. Another legal document proving she would get the money back. Except it turned out that Beth was not Don's legal wife. Don had already been married when he married Beth. This new issue opened up another wound. Beth could not believe this turn of events and crumbled to the floor in sobs. She had become used to the idea that her money would never be recovered. She suspected he had left the country to set up a new life somewhere. But the knowledge of his death and the discovery of her funds had given her new hope.

For several weeks, she had been on a high assuming that her financial problems would soon be long gone once all the red tape was taken care of. The new information that Don had already been married when he married her cut her to the core. It meant that their relationship was a scam from start to finish; that there had never been any attraction or love from him; that the whole scenario had been carefully calculated and she had fallen for it all. He would have gotten away with it, too, if someone hadn't wanted him dead. Beth didn't know who, but then she had to admit she knew nothing about the man she had innocently married. She returned to New York more depressed than ever before.

This recent blow to her self-esteem did not help her overall mental health. To feel better, she turned to Quench. There, she could have sex without the pretense that someone cared for her. The venue gave her just what she needed, a place for sex and nothing more, and that was fine with her. Her engagement in sex became riskier. Hell, she had nothing to lose. She never gave a thought to her health or reputation. Years ago, she had been thought of as a beautiful, somewhat shy, sex partner but now, she had the reputation of being dirty and not worth the risk. Those at Quench were no longer attracted to the woman whose reputation was as sullied as she was. Men wouldn't trust someone who didn't care if they wore a condom or if they ever had a medical checkup. To remain sexually active, Beth joined swingers off the Quench premises in scuzzy hotel rooms and private homes where drugs and booze kept everyone going.

Beth was careful to keep her clean image for work – she would not risk losing her job. With the holiday season upon them, the Golden Grain staff were run off their feet preparing for and serving at one holiday party after the other. The Christmas and Hanukah parties were often family-themed, but once New Year's Eve came, it was adult only. The wealthy New Yorkers knew how to throw a glitzy affair.

Beth and her crew were hired to cater such a party. It was held in a very large, million dollar Manhattan penthouse. The gourmet kitchen was a caterer's dream with yards of counter space, multiple sinks, dishwashers and refrigerators. Ellis, the owner was both surprised and pleased to see that Beth was part of the evening's catering staff. He made it clear that once she was finished serving his guests, he wanted her to serve him – privately. As she recalled, her previous rendezvous with Ellis included high-quality cocaine among other things and he seemed to relish life on the edge. Throughout the night, whenever he got the chance, he would tap her on the bottom or fondle her breast, making it difficult, at times, to balance her tray or pour the champagne; but it definitely kept her interest. Near the end of the night, Ellis slipped Beth five, one hundred dollar bills. Some would have considered the money as payment for an upcoming sexual tryst, but Beth rationalized it as a tip for the great job she did serving his guests.

Beth continued bringing trays of caviar, smoked salmon, truffles and a host of other finger foods as the evening wore on. She was becoming familiar with the guests and their preferences when she noticed the butler ushering in a small group of people. She waited until he had taken their coats, then politely approached them to take their drink orders. The guests turned to face her causing her to inhale sharply. One of the guests was none other than Tom Ricci from Kendrick. He was obviously as shocked to see her as she was to run into him. Neither let on to anyone else that they were acquainted, but both knew they would talk before the party ended.

Eventually, getting Beth alone in the kitchen, Tom explained that Rosa was not with him and that they lived apart. Rosa had moved in with Sam, and Tom admitted he had finally had enough and had completed divorce proceedings. He had heard rumors at the club about her and Don and wondered how much was true compared to the gossip that ran rampant. Sadly, Beth had confirmed that most of what Tom had heard was true. With the details confirmed, he knew he had so much more to say to her, to discuss with her, to offer her and he told her so. His phone rang just then, and looking at the display, he saw it was a call he needed to take. He excused himself with an apology, promising to find her again as soon as he could. He made his way to Ellis's study where there would be some quiet privacy.

Beth kept a look out for Tom, but each time she entered the living room from the kitchen, he was nowhere in sight. She could tell by his demeanor that what he had to say was urgent and she needed to find out what it was. A half hour passed, and many of the guests had begun to leave. At this point, Beth was trying to dodge Ellis. She knew she had promised him a fling, and she had a feeling he would want that promise fulfilled sooner than later. She was right. Out of the blue, she felt arms encircling her waist from behind. She knew Tom wouldn't be so forward; it had to be Ellis. Without a word, he led her by the hand to his master suite. As Ellis closed the door behind them, Beth could see that the study door, down the hall, remained shut. She hoped Tom would not leave before they had a chance to talk again.

While Tom was taking his phone call, Beth was getting wasted on the cocaine that Ellis was helping to spoon up her nose, and the vodka martinis he was generously pouring. They sat on his California King, which was dwarfed by the immense grand, master suite. White, plush carpeting, and white, clean-lined contemporary furnishings, adorned the room. Steel gray walls with glossy white crown moldings, door frames, and base boards outlined and softened the dark walls. The room was dimly lit with recessed lighting from the ceiling and headboard of Ellis's bed, as well as crystal lamps – all of which could be controlled with the touch of a remote.

Centered over the bed hung two, white, paddle fans, controlled by the remote not only for fan speed, but for lowering the fans from the cathedral ceiling for more direct cooling.

"I have something special planned for you tonight," said Ellis with a wink.

"What?" laughed Beth, sucking down her martini.

"Take off your clothes, and I will show you."

"Okay," giggled Beth. She tried kneeling, but fell over as she rolled around on his bed trying to get her uniform off. "I'm kinda tipsy. Hey! Where are you? Ellis?"

"I'm back," said a naked Ellis as he walked back to the bed carrying a piece of rope and two pairs of handcuffs. He tossed them down beside Beth and opened his night stand drawer, pulling out drug paraphernalia. He placed it on the night stand and turned his attention to Beth.

Beth just stared at Ellis. *Here we go again with bondage. Don hated being restrained,* thought Beth.

"What's with the syringe and drugs?" asked Beth, already knowing the answer.

"Heroin – for me, not you. So, don't worry."

"I take it you want to tie me up and fuck me?"

"Not exactly," said Ellis slyly. "What do you know about erotic asphyxiation?" he asked Beth.

"It involves compressing the carotid arteries during sexual stimulation, causing increased levels of carbon dioxide to accumulate in the brain. Feelings of giddiness and heightened sexual sensations occur," laughed Beth.

"Well, Dr. Waitress, that's quite an astute explanation," replied Ellis.

Beth ignored Ellis's snide comment, not bothering to explain that she used to be a nurse practitioner. He saw her as nothing. *I am nothing. I have nothing,* thought Beth.

"I'll go first, then you. You're going to love it. Nothing beats the intensity."

Ellis grabbed the remote and lowered one fan. He stood on the bed and securely tied one end of the rope to its long shaft. The other end of the rope had already been fashioned into a noose. He knelt on his knees and slipped the noose around his neck checking for proper rope length, allowing no slack.

"This should be fine. Here's what's going to happen. Put the handcuffs on my wrists behind my back, as well as the ankle restraints. The key is right there," he said pointing to the small silver key, as he tightened the noose. "I want you to give me head, and at the point of orgasm, I'm going to sink down from my knees choking myself out. Then you un-cuff me and get the noose off me. Not necessarily in that order!" laughed Ellis. "Oh, and if anything goes wrong with the rope – there is a sharp knife in the night stand drawer."

"Why do we need to restrain our ankles?" asked Beth with a slight slur, but trying to concentrate.

"Otherwise we could just stand up."

What the hell? Thought Beth. *Then I can go find Tom.*

"Got it," said Beth as she moved behind him and handcuffed his wrists as instructed. She sat down Indian style in front of him and grabbed his semi-erect cock. Her heart was racing from the coke, and she was feeling buzzed from the vodka. Slipping her mouth over him, she sucked his cock while running her tongue around the head. Her right hand joined her mouth, pulling and firmly twisting around the base of his rod. She took her mouth off and pumped him up and down with her hand before sticking out her tongue and flicking the underside, then swirling around the swollen head of his cock once again.

Beth heard Ellis's breathing become more rapid, signaling he was getting close to cuming. His eyes were closed in concentration, but he was starting to relax his knees. Beth slid her mouth up and down, vigorously sucking and licking, faster and faster until she heard Ellis choking and felt him convulse and fall away from her while spraying his cum on the way down. Beth immediately grabbed the remote and lowered the fan. The noose was now loose enough to remove. She rolled him to the side, unlocked and tossed aside the cuffs. Beth pushed him to his back and slapped at his face, watching the purplish-red color slowly fade as he gasped for air and opened his eyes.

"That is scary as shit to watch!" exclaimed Beth when Ellis was able to sit back up.

He crawled to the head of the bed and leaned against the pillows. He sipped on his drink, and said to Beth, "That was killer. Are you ready?"

"I guess so." *It didn't take him long, so I should be out of here in ten,* thought Beth.

Beth got into position, and Ellis took up the rope slightly because of the difference in their height. Unlike the instructions he had requested for himself, he handcuffed Beth's wrists in front of her, then her ankles behind her. He leaned over the edge of the bed and pulled out a second length of cotton rope. He wrapped the rope around her, well below her breasts, pinning her arms in front of her at the elbows. She raised her eyebrows and asked why.

"I want to watch you masturbate, but I don't want you to panic and pull the noose off too soon."

Wanting to get it over with, Beth separated her lips with her left hand and, with short restricted movements, began to stimulate her clit with the first two fingers of her right hand. She certainly wasn't feeling very horny with a noose around her neck; all she wanted to do was come down from the high she was feeling.

Ellis sat back and heated his heroin on a spoon and drew it up into the syringe. He deftly wrapped a tourniquet around his arm and injected into a prominent vein. He sat back, unwrapped the tourniquet, and watched Beth through heavy eyelids and glazed over eyes.

"Yeah, baby. Play with your clit," Ellis said slowly with slurred speech before he slumped over.

"Ellis, Ellis! Oh, God!" exclaimed Beth, which sounded like a forced, hoarse whisper from her constricted throat.

In her panic, Beth's sudden, jerky movements caused her to lose her balance, like a fallen tree, tightening the noose around her neck.

I'm going to die here, naked and handcuffed like some animal! Please, Tom, rescue me! Why aren't you looking for me? Oh my God – Matt and Max. I hope Jack and Cindy never tell them how I died. We never told them about Richard's suicide, and they needn't know the embarrassment of their mother either. I remember the look in Richard's eyes when the Labor & Delivery nurses handed him each of his sons for the first time. He was such a proud and wonderful father. Why did I ever agree to go to Club Climax? If I had said no, Richard would be alive, and we would be happy living our boring American dream in Kendrick. I'm so sleepy. I can't see or hear anything. I think it's happening. I'm really dying.

As Beth slipped deeper into unconsciousness, her brain replayed her fears of several years ago regarding their first visit to Club Climax. *Once again, she went over the decision-making process that had taken place so long ago. How did she get talked into this? She understood full well how...a couple of cocktails and a smooth-talking husband – that's how! Ever since she had reluctantly agreed to this plan, Richard had had this little twinkle in his eye, and she knew he was looking forward to it with every fiber of his being, particularly those masculine fibers. She felt she just couldn't back out. He would be so disappointed. But a sex club? She could vaguely imagine Richard at one but couldn't begin to visualize herself there.*

The call Tom received was from his family. His three kids, their spouses, and his grandchildren had all taken a luxurious ski vacation into the Canadian Rockies. The differing time zones made it early on the West Coast but past midnight in New York. Once Tom had talked to each of the kids and then to all the grandchildren, Rosa had snatched the phone. There was no good cheer or Happy New Year's Eve wishes from her, just venomous words that insulted him and tried to make him feel guilty about not being with his family. He might have agreed to go along except that his ex-wife had invited her boyfriend on the trip, and that was where he drew the line.

Tom ended up hanging up on Rosa when she would not talk civilly to him. He placed the phone into his pocket and left the study. His first thought was to find Beth, so he could continue their conversation, which he hoped would end in a marriage proposal or at least an agreement to begin their relationship, once again.

For years, from the first time Tom had met Beth, he had wanted her. He remembered how nervous and seemingly naïve she had been on her and husband Richard's first visit to the club. He had taken her under his wing, that night, as he and Rosa had led the tour for Club Climax virgins. Much had happened between them, and to them, since then and he knew both of them sported recent scars. Beth had gone from being the most compatible lover he had ever enjoyed to meaning much more to him than just good sex. He had fallen in love with her long ago and to this day hoped they could somehow get together.

It was time for Tom to tell Beth how much he loved her, how much he had always loved her. She needed to know he was divorced now and finally free to ask her to marry him. He couldn't wait to see the look on her face! He was just as excited to marry Beth as he was to help her raise those two fantastic little boys. But where the hell was she?

Tom opened and closed multiple doors down the hallway, calling out Beth's name. He finally came to the end of the hallway, and pushed open the double doors to Ellis's master suite. He didn't believe what his eyes were telling his brain! *Dear God, not my Beth!* He ran and leaped onto the bed, pulling up Beth's limp body so that he could loosen the noose. He couldn't look at her purple face, so he kept his eyes on her neck and the rope that was finally loose enough to pull over her head.

"Call 911! Call 911!" Tom shouted, hoping the cleaning staff had heard him.

"Beth, baby. Wake up, wake up!"

Tom glanced over to Ellis and didn't know if he was alive or dead, and he didn't care.

He knew CPR, but first he un-cuffed Beth's wrists and ankles. He didn't waste time trying to untie the rope from around Beth's torso and arms. She had a pulse, thank God, but she wasn't breathing.

He breathed into Beth's mouth, praying silently to see her chest move on its own. He kept breathing for her until he heard the paramedics running down the hall. They burst into the room, pushing Tom away from Beth, and began attending to her. He stepped into the hallway, leaned against the wall and slid down to the polished marble floor, sobbing. As he slumped onto the floor, he overhead one of the paramedics say Ellis was dead – 'overdose'.

Are you punishing me, God? Punish me then, not her. She's a good woman. Please, save her, so I can make up for all the wrong.

The fifty thousand dollars Tom had offered Don's assassin had been rejected. The killer had said he didn't require money to rid the world of filth; the satisfaction of someone like Don being dead was enough. Tom wished the killer he had hired to take care of Richard had shared the same altruistic attitude. Hell, Richard had killed himself, but the hired hitman had kept the money – standard operating procedure for that line of work.

Tom would have paid twice the money to keep Beth safe from those trying to hurt her. He knew how to cover his tracks, and Beth would never find out that he had been responsible for erasing the two biggest problems from her life. He would take care of her from now on, and she would have no reason to ever doubt his love or wonder to what extent he would go to make her his.

Chapter 23

Beth awoke to the sounds of beeping monitors, hospital smells, and the feel of oxygen being blown into her nostrils. She fluttered her eyelids, and squinted at the bright, fluorescent lighting above her. Feeling a warm hand squeezing her own, she turned her head to see Tom looking at her with the tender, loving expression that she remembered so well.

"Oh, Tom," was all Beth could say before the tears ran down her face, and sobs shook her thin body.

"Shh. It's okay. Everything is going to be okay. You and I are going to be together forever. I'm never going to leave you. I love you, Beth."

The nurse, having impeccable timing, walked in and said, "Hi, Beth. How are you feeling?"

"Embarrassed, but I couldn't be happier. Thank you."

"Well, we're glad you're going to make a full recovery. Your knight in shining armor here saved your life. I'll be back in a minute. Your doc will want to know that you're awake."

Beth waited for her to leave the room and said, "Tom, is that true? You saved me? I was praying for you to find me!"

"Well, I walked in at the right time, that's all. Please don't cry, babe."

"I can't help it," sobbed Beth.

Tom stood up and sat on the edge of her hospital bed

and held her tight, letting her cry her heart out.

"I love you so much, Tom," Beth whispered toward his neck. *Richard, if you're looking down, know that I am okay. Your fears about Tom were wrong. He's a wonderful man. He will help raise our boys, and I know he will be an excellent role model and provider. You can rest in peace.*

"And you know I love you," replied Tom. "I always have, always will. You and the boys will never have to worry. I will always keep you safe."

Beth and Tom looked deeply into each other's eyes while Richard's spirit had never felt so uneasy.

QUENCH - Drink Recipes
Cocktails

1. **Mistress Maggie's Melon Mash**
   1 ½ oz. watermelon vodka
   1 ½ oz. mango-pineapple flavored vodka
   Fresca and a splash of grenadine

2. **Rosanna's Banana Leg Split**
   1 ½ oz. crème de banana
   1 ½ oz. Irish cream
   Layer in glass and serve

3. **6 Feet Under**
   1 oz. lemon vodka
   1 oz. melon liqueur
   1 oz. coconut rum
   Splash of sweet 'n sour mix and 7-Up

4. **Cherry Popper**
   1 oz. cherry schnapps
   Fill with 7-Up
   Add the cherry!

5. **Juicy Fruit Cocktail**
   1 oz. rainbow sherbet vodka
   ½ oz. melon liqueur
   ½ oz. peach schnapps
   Fill with pineapple juice

6. **S'more Please**
   2 oz. S'more vodka
   1 oz. chocolate liqueur
   1 oz. Irish cream
   Shake and serve over ice

7. **John Juan**
1 ½ oz. root beer vodka
1 ½ oz. vanilla liqueur
Fill with cream

8. **Rimmer**
Rim glass with shaved chocolate
2 oz. bacon-infused rye whisky
½ oz. sweet vermouth
3 dashes of bitters
Garnish with bacon dipped in chocolate
 & sea salt

9. **Hot Ass**
4 oz. Fire Puncher Vodka
Hot sauce to taste
Slice of jalapeno pepper

10. **Moran's Purple Passion**
4 oz. vodka
2 oz. each of pineapple, grape, and orange juice
Slice of lime and a cherry

11. **Tea Bagger**
2 oz. fruit loops vodka
Iced tea

12. **Jizz Fizz**
1 ½ oz. vodka
1 ½ oz. white rum
Irish cream

QUENCH - Drink Recipes
Martinis

13. The Lifestyle Signature Martini
4 oz. Krug Champaign
2 oz. Goldschlagger schnapps
Cinnamon heart garnish

14. Dirty Martini
2 ½ oz. gin
½ oz. dry vermouth
¼ oz. olive juice
Olive

15. Birthday Suit Martini
Rim glass with sprinkles
2 oz. birthday cake vodka
2 oz. amaretto
½ oz. white chocolate liqueur
2 oz. half and half cream
Garnish with whip cream and sprinkles

16. Knotty Martini
3 oz. fireweed vodka
¼ oz. violette liqueur
1 oz. white grape juice
Shake, strain, and pour

17. Blow Me Martini
2 oz. bubble gum vodka
Splash of sour watermelon
2 oz. strong lemonade
Garnish with a blow pop

18.   **Hit the Hole Martini**
       2 oz. glazed donut vodka
       2 oz. crème de cacao
       1 oz. vanilla syrup
       2 oz. half and half cream

Please Drink Responsibly

The Authors:

R Conté is the pen name of one half of the Conté writing duo. This retired nurse practitioner lives in southwestern Pennsylvania and enjoys writing, golf, the beach, trail-walking with her husband and a good glass of wine!

M Conté represents the second author of the writing partnership. She works as a nurse practitioner in western Pennsylvania. In her free time, she enjoys writing dark poetry, taking beach vacations with her family and attempting to master the game of golf.

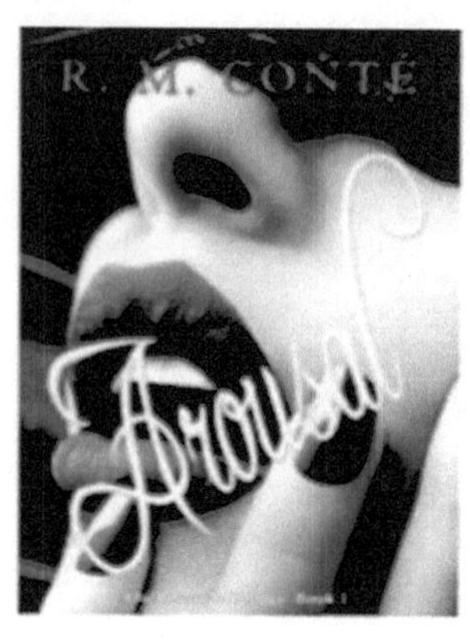

Title: Arousal

The Lifestyle Trilogy

- Author: R M Conté
- Publisher: TotalRecall Publications, Inc.
- Paper Back: ISBN: 9781590954546
- eBook: ISBN: 9781590954553
- Number of pages in the finished book: 352
- Publication Date: August 4, 2015

Richard and Beth Anderson, upper, middle-class parents in their late thirties, warily accept a friend's invitation to visit a swingers' club. Several visits later, they realize they enjoy the lifestyle and become members of Club Climax. The Club provides them a venue for the hottest sex of their lives with each other, with their friends and with strangers. Unfortunately, what goes on at the Club is not all good, clean fun as Richard discovers. Becoming friends with an unsavory couple and the poor choices that result, brings turmoil to many aspects of his life including his marriage, work as an architect and his very existence.

Beth has issues of her own. Mutual, smoldering, sexual tension between her and wealthy club member, Tom, results in lustful, yet sensual love-making that delights the Club's voyeurs. Their private, penthouse, sexual explosions break the swinger code of conduct and cause Beth to become deceitful to those around her.

Once happily married and devoted parents, the Andersons become caught up in the lifestyle which serves to unbalance their priorities and destroy the serene, predictable life they once enjoyed. Can they get 'happily ever after' back?

Title: **Obsession**

The Lifestyle Trilogy

- Author: R M Conté
- Publisher: TotalRecall Publications, Inc.
- Paper Back: ISBN: 9781590954935
- eBook: ISBN: 9781590954942
- Number of pages in the finished book: 360
- Publication Date: September 8, 2015

Beth Anderson, a recently widowed mother of two, finds solace in her swinger lifestyle. When friends invite her on a swingers' cruise her intention is to relax and enjoy the Caribbean sun. Unexpectedly, fellow swinger Don, a wealthy business owner becomes the man of her dreams. As their relationship quickly intensifies, Beth ignores her friends' complaints that their relationship is moving too quickly at the expense of her sons. Tom, a dear friend and lover from the past, wants her to himself and sets out to discredit Beth's new love interest by exposing his flaws.

Despite the phenomenal sex she and Don enjoy when together, Beth becomes tired of dealing with the annoyances and issues their long-distance relationship causes as well as with the criticism and interference of friends who say she is obsessed with her new boyfriend. Her concerns come to a head and she feels forced to make a decision about their tenuous relationship. Their distressing conversation leads to a final decision. Did Beth choose wisely?